MRS. WATSON AND THE DEATH CULT

When the body of a prominent businessman is found floating in an ancient Roman bath, all the evidence points to a young man named Ronald Standish as the murderer. His wife appeals to her old governess Amelia, the second wife of Dr. John H. Watson, for help. Soon, Amelia is thrust into a baffling mystery involving the practice of ancient pagan religious rites in the modern city of Bath. At every step, though, she finds evidence that makes the case against Standish even stronger . . .

MICHAEL MALLORY

MRS. WATSON AND THE DEATH CULT

Complete and Unabridged

LINFORD
Leicester

First published in Great Britain

First Linford Edition
published 2017

A catalogue record for this book is available
from the British Library.

ISBN 978–1–4448–3276–1

Published by
F. A. Thorpe (Publishing)
Anstey, Leicestershire

Set by Words & Graphics Ltd.
Anstey, Leicestershire
Printed and bound in Great Britain by
T. J. International Ltd., Padstow, Cornwall

This book is printed on acid-free paper

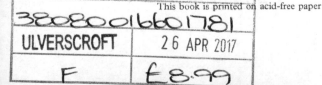

Prologue:

The group of men gathered in darkness at the edge of an ancient oak grove near the southerly curve of the River Avon, far from the gaze of those inhabiting the stately Georgian houses that were terraced upon the nearby hills. Normally they were twelve, but on this night only eleven donned the long, white, hooded robes, which were not only necessary for the ceremony, but also protected them against the chill. Above them, the full moon bathed the wood in an eerie blue light.

The men were there to carry out their ancient rites: ceremonies older than the city of Bath, older than the trees around them, perhaps even older than England itself.

Another figure now appeared: the priest, who, in contrast to the dove-white robes

1

of the celebrants, wore a cope covered in shimmering green and blue sequins, representing the scales of a water creature, and a cloth mask depicting a fish-like face enwreathed by a mane of wild, splayed hair. Standing on a long, flat stone that had been laboriously transported to the spot too long ago to remember, the priest called for the multitude to form a circle around the stone at its head.

'We gather here, oh exalted Cam,' the priest began, 'with the desire that you might look upon us, your devoted followers, with charity and pity. Grant us, oh Great One, the continued honour of serving you.'

The eleven in the circle repeated the words.

'Pity us, oh Great One, that we are too weak of mind and spirit to comprehend the extent of your eminence.'

The worshippers again echoed him.

'Through your blessed charity, permit us to thrive and prosper in our lives that we may continue to dedicate our souls and wills to you.'

The responding chant was delivered with great sincerity, with emphasis on the words 'thrive' and 'prosper' from the multitude.

'Through your great puissance we derive our own strength and potency.'

The response echoed with enthusiasm.

'Grant us the strength to combat your enemies, those who would deny your supremacy over the world, trample your sacred name, and attempt to force unholy beliefs on those of us who serve you.'

Adorned in his priest's robes, George Frankham, businessman of the city of Bath, continued to recite the ritual, though largely by rote. His thoughts were instead centered on Ronald Standish and the unpleasantness that had taken place between them the previous day. *Damn him*, Frankham thought bitterly. *Damn him for what he is.* Standish was nothing but a commoner, an unbeliever, an ignorant whelp that dared to talk to him as an equal, who had even dared to threaten him! *Damn him to the abyss!* Frankham silently raged.

Forcing his mind back on the ceremony, Frankham bade that the circle of men be broken, the signal that the ceremony was coming to an end. 'Let no one whose eyes are clouded with the sty of misunderstanding see us,' he intoned. 'Let no one whose ears are closed against the truth hear us. Let no one whose heart is blackened and withered stand in the way of the light of the true believer. Let darkness be our cloak against the unbelievers.'

As he spoke the final invocation, he offered a silent prayer of his own: *Great Being, Almighty Cam, destroy the heart and soul of Ronald Standish; take him down into the dark waters with you where he might never escape; rid the earth of his pestilence.*

Stepping down from the stone, Frankham bade the celebrants, 'Go in service to our exalted Lord Cam.' None of the eleven spoke. No one ever spoke after a ceremony, though Frankham knew he would be seeing at least half of the men here in the daylight in the city before the week was out.

All was silent now, silent except for the sonorous chirping of the crickets in the woods and the steady rush of the river Avon as it coursed past the ceremonial spot. The smells of earth and woods combined to make a strangely seductive scent, and not for the first time after a ceremony,

Frankham was aware of how heightened his senses had become. He was ravenously hungry, and suddenly desirous of a woman.

Under the light of the full moon, George Frankham made his way through the woods to the spot where a leather bag, a bit larger than a doctor's medical case, was hidden. He opened it and pulled out his suit coat, which had been carefully folded and put inside, and absently reminded himself that he had to get his other coat fixed. He quickly removed his sequinned robe and mask and stuffed them inside the bag. Donning his coat, he took up the bag, and started out on the three-quarter mile walk toward the city.

Some of the others had carriages waiting for them at the edge of the woods, held in place by trusted servants. But Frankham trusted no one, servile or otherwise, and felt that those who did were fools, practically begging for betrayal. Besides, he enjoyed these night walks, feeling the crisp sting of the evening air on his face and the pleasant stretch of his legs, while taking the chance to ruminate about the ceremony, or anything else that was happening in his life at that time.

The stained-glass façade of Bath Abbey, which glowed like an enormous flame against the night sky, was clearly visible even before Frankham had reached the southern gate of the city. The sight brought a grimace to his face. Purely as a monument, the abbey was nothing short of spectacular. But it never failed to strike Frankham as a garish, if not ostentatious, edifice to a false god. How many fools had been lead astray by the troublemaking Hebrew philosopher in whose name it was consecrated? How many had gone to their graves still clinging to the belief in a salvation that was as false as the medieval construct of the universe? In regards to the most extreme irony, how many realised that the fish symbol that had represented their glorified prophet since ancient times was really a stolen and bastardised icon of the Great One Himself?

How Almighty Cam must be laughing at the folly of mankind.

It was quarter past one in the morning by the time George Frankham had made his way to Stall Street, which headed towards the Great Bath. That was the one aspect of the ceremonies that he would have liked to change, the fact that they did not even begin until midnight. But that could hardly be altered. It was, in fact, rather the point.

His fashionable house in Ashdown Crescent, on the northern slope of the city, was still a good twenty minutes away, but he could shorten his walk by cutting through the courtyard of the abbey and past the ancient ruins of the Great Bath. The ruins held a fascination for him. The bath had been built by the Romans during their occupation of Britain, around the sacred spring of Cam, which even then was ageless — not that they truly recognised its significance, of course. No, the Romans had simply been the first in a long line of conquerors to believe that their state-supported religion would supplant the Old Gods, the Original Gods, the True Gods. They, of course, learned of their folly, just as the Christians who had supplanted them would someday learn of theirs.

The front of the abbey rose before Frankham like the prow of a majestic ship. How much longer, he wondered, would it be before it too fell into the earth, like these powerful ancient Roman ruins, only to be rediscovered again and considered quaint by future generations? How much longer before the long-buried, long-ignored Old Gods returned to hold dominion over the rampant vulgarity of the new Twentieth Century?

George Frankham savoured the thought, alone in the glow of the sham abbey.

Alone — or so he thought.

A noise came from the other side of the stone wall that separated the terrace surrounding the Great Bath from the abbey courtyard. Then another noise carried through the still, dark night: the sound of footsteps.

Someone was on the terrace.

Frankham's initial reaction was to turn and flee, but he fought the urge down. After all, he had done nothing wrong. There was no city curfew, and except for his private thoughts, he was not vandalizing the sacred grounds of the abbey in any way. Chances were excellent that he had already been seen by whoever it was — most likely a constable keeping watch over the area — and all he would accomplish by running away was to cast unnecessary suspicion over him. It would be better to be seen in all his innocence.

Frankham approached the terrace wall. 'Is anyone up there?' he called out.

A faint voice came back. 'Thank God,' it moaned. 'Help me ... please help me.'

How typical, Frankham thought. Whenever fools got in trouble, they invoked the god of the Christists, yet it was not 'God' who would come to the rescue — it never was — but rather he, George Frankham, true believer. He had half a mind to walk away and leave the unfortunate to the whims of a false deity.

'For God's sake ... help me,' continued the voice, which might have belonged to either a man or a woman.

What if it were a woman? Frankham thought suddenly. *How grateful would the wench be?* Grateful enough, perhaps, to do anything for him in return ...

'Are you in distress?' Frankham called.

'Yes ... please come ...'

He still could not tell the gender of the person from the voice, but decided to take the chance that it was a woman.

'I am coming.'

The terrace surrounding the Great Bath was elevated about six feet above the street level and surrounded by a wall. Setting down his bag on its side, he used it as a step as he gripped the wall and began to clamber up. It was not a difficult climb, but he had barely swung a leg over the top before he began feeling foolish. How on earth had the bitch got up here in the first place? Probably the same way as Frankham just had — a thought that prompted him to take special care stepping down from the wall, lest he end up in trouble himself. Even though there was an inner railing on the terrace, the Bath was two full storeys below, a formidable drop should he accidentally fall.

Frankham called: 'Where are you?' but only received a moan in return. It came from the corner of the terrace.

Using the inner rail as a guide, he moved towards the sound, gazing as he walked into the dark, hidden waters below. But when he reached the corner, there was no sign of anyone else.

'I cannot see you.'

'I am here,' the voice said, now so close

behind him that Frankham gasped. He spun around in time to see a dark figure. 'Is this some perverse sort of game?' he demanded.

'It is all a game, is it not?' the figure replied, and then swung a wooden cudgel against Frankham's temple, toppling him forward. His assailant brought the cudgel down again, this time on the back of his neck, sending a fiery bolt of pain through his head.

Too stunned to rise, Frankham could feel himself being pulled upwards, hefted onto the stone rail over the Bath, and rested there. 'Damn you,' he managed to utter, though the effort nearly caused him to pass out. The next thing he felt was the sensation of his legs being lifted behind him.

'No,' Frankham pleaded, but it was too late. His assailant shoved his legs forward and Frankham plummeted over the railing and into the dark abyss. Hitting the surface of the water with a slap, George Frankham's last conscious thought was that the God of the Waters had inexplicably betrayed him. He attempted to breathe, but instead of air, he drew into his lungs the warm, stinging, ancient water of the Bath. All movement then stopped, and the Bath accepted his body into itself, then settled and smoothed over the top of him.

Up above on the terrace, the dark figure crept back towards the outer wall, carefully slid over, and climbed down to the empty courtyard of the abbey, landing on top of something at the street level. Closer inspection revealed it to be the black bag that Frankham had carried from the ceremony. Picking it up, the shadowy figure hastened into the cool, enveloping arms of the night; unseen, unheard, undiscovered.

1

CHAPTER XIII

Then, gracious reader, the heavy, lead-coloured clouds that had obscured the sky like a curtain for most of that day parted to reveal what rational men on that night would have wagered was there all along, even though they could not have seen it: the moon! The pregnant yellow orb gleamed like a golden beacon high above the mortal earth, causing ominous shadows to be cast by the ancient stones that spread over the deserted expanse of the plain of Salisbury. Into this spider's web of faded light and umbrous shadow ran the fair Felicity, her diaphanous gown wafting behind her like a woven puff of smoke. Roaring across the plain behind her came the venomous form of Lord D'Arbany himself, atop a hellish black steed, his lips stretched into a hellish grimace, his red eyes piercing the night like two glowing coals and, worst of all, the Druid dagger clenched tightly in his talon-like fist.

Quivering in fear, the girl vociferated: 'Oh, Heaven help me! Send a saviour to rescue me from this vile wretch!'

'No one can help you!' Lord D'Arbany crowed, and followed his words with a stridulous laugh.

Gripped with breathless panic, Felicity attempted to run, but given her haste and weakened condition, she instead stumbled and fell against the tallest trilithon of the massive and enigmatic stone circle. Looking up, she saw the sallow moon-drenched face of Lord D'Arbany looming over her, the ancient dagger clenched in his upraised hand. 'This very night shall be your last!' he intoned, leaping down from the midnight stallion. 'Oh, my grace; oh, my gazelle; oh, my Galatea —'

'Oh my God,' I moaned, snapping the book closed and shuddering, not at the villainy of Lord D'Arbany, but at the far more heinous crime perpetrated upon the reading public by the author. 'Missy,' I called to our young maid, 'is this really the best you were able to find at the lending library?'

14

'Mum, the man said *The Full Flowering of Felicity* was his most popular book,' she replied. 'He said there was a waiting list for it, and that I was lucky to get it at all.'

Missy Trelawney had been with us for nearly two years now, during which time I have done my best to oversee her transformation from a timid, bashful girl to a slightly more poised young woman. Even though our house was on the small side (though not disproportionately so as compared with the other houses on London's Queen Anne Street), there was one room to spare, which Missy occupied. However, while her assurance as a young woman had grown somewhat, her taste in literature had not, despite my best efforts to educate her. I had a strong suspicion that Mr. Hedgepeth, the proprietor of the Charing Cross lending library, had recommended the book by sizing up the girl and selecting a title he thought would suit her, not realizing she had been sent to find something that would suit me.

I would have gone myself if not for my wretched ankle, which I had severely sprained while attempting to scamper out

15

of the path of a roaring motorcar that was about to overtake me. Those mechanical nightmares were increasingly invading the streets, yet another sign of the infernal 'progress' of the new century. Climbing stairs had been a near-impossibility for the last week, forcing me to venture no further than to and from bedroom and day room. The only positive element in this wealth of negatives is the fact that my husband is a doctor, and has been able to offer private treatment at all hours of the night and day.

In fact, I believe I am at present John's only patient, most of his time being taken up with other matters.

As gently as possible, I lifted myself off the chaise until I had achieved a standing position, and began to test how much weight my foot would bear. From across the room, John glanced up from his writing desk, a stern look on his handsome face.

'Amelia, you are not supposed to be up,' he cautioned. 'Tell either Missy or I what it is you want, and we shall get it for you.'

'What I want is to be able to leave this house,' I said.

'You shouldn't really be walking on it yet.'

'Really, darling, it is far less painful now than it was, and certainly less painful than the writing in *The Full Flowering of Felicity*.' Turning to our maid, I added: 'Please take this back and exchange it for another, Missy.'

'Very well, mum,' she responded, taking the book and flouncing out of the room.

'The girl's taste in literature is positively subterranean,' I told my husband.

'I am glad that I do not let you read my manuscripts before they are sent to the publishers,' he replied.

'Nonsense, John. It is because of your literary skills that Sherlock Holmes has become a household name. The reading public at large greets each new instalment in the continuing saga of Sherlock Holmes, from the pen of his personal friend and confidant Dr. John H. Watson, with bouquets. You have turned Mr. Holmes into such a celebrity that I hear the prime minister is thinking of changing the name of the Home Office to the *Holmes* Office.'

'Now you are mocking me, Amelia.'

I was, of course, though I also happened to believe every word. Not only are his chronicles of the cases of his former flat-mate vividly and colourfully written, he has managed to take a moody, maddening, misogynistic, and thoroughly inscrutable misanthrope and turn him into a popular hero. 'I am sorry, John, please forgive — *ah!*'

In my attempt to take a step towards him, my foot had suddenly turned inward, sending a fiery arrow of pain through my ankle and causing me to lose my balance. John sprang out of his chair as though he had been catapulted, and caught me before I fell to the floor.

Missy dashed back in, asking: 'What is it, mum?'

'She has overtaxed her ankle again,' John said. 'Missy, please go down to the fish-monger's and see if you can get a bucket of ice. A cold compress will help the healing process.'

Once the girl had gone on her errand, I turned back to my husband and moaned: 'Must I really be confined to this couch for another week?'

'That depends on how stationary you can

18

become,' he said. 'If you can force yourself to remain here for another day, possibly two, and be sure to put the ice on your ankle every hour or so, you could be up and around by the end of the week.'

'Thank heavens for that!' I declared. 'Just sitting here, staring at the same four walls day in and day out, is excruciating.'

John smiled as he began re-bandaging my foot. 'You know, Amelia, you almost sound like Holmes when you say that. Neither of you are equipped to cope with boredom. It is what drove him to the needle.'

I groaned again. 'Now I suppose you are going to begin relating to me as if I were he!'

'Hardly,' he said, softly, before kissing me.

★   ★   ★

Whether a result of the ice or my self-enforced inactivity, I was indeed back on my feet — if a trifle wobbly — within three days, as John had predicted. I was, however, being forced to continue my recuperation on my own, since John had responded to an emergency call from an agent to replace a fellow who had been engaged for a lecture tour through Scotland, but was forced to cancel due to illness. Since John was ready to speak about his escapades with Sherlock Holmes at a moment's notice, and the money being offered was not much less than his annual military pension, he jumped at the chance. He had left this very morning, promising to send me letters from the road.

It was the missive that had arrived in the afternoon post, though, that was occupying my thoughts at the moment. Amid the bills was an envelope addressed to me from a Mrs. R. Standish, Victoria Buildings, Albert Street, Bath; which was odd, to say the least, since I knew no one in that city. I tore into the envelope and pulled from it two sheets of paper, which I unfolded. A faint trace of rose water wafted up from the paper as I read:

Dear Mrs. Watson:
  I doubt that you will remember me, but when I was a child you were Miss Pettigrew, my governess. My name

then was Bella Mabry and I was the daughter of the rector of Lewes. You came to us when I was nine and stayed for a little over a year.

Good heavens, little Bella! Shutting my eyes, I could still picture her: a small, if somewhat round, child with enormous, dark, almost frightened eyes, and a kind of neediness in her personality that I ascribed to her having lost her mother at a young age.

I went back to the letter:

Needless to say, I have grown since last seeing you. I am now the wife of Ronald Standish, who is a wonderful man and husband, and who has been trying to launch a career as an architect and builder here in Bath. But Ronnie has managed to get himself into horrible trouble through no fault of his own. He is currently in jail, being charged with murder.

'Good God,' I muttered.

I am writing to you out of desperation. I have recently learned, much to my surprise, that you are the wife of Dr. Watson, the friend of Sherlock Holmes. Miss Petti— (The last two words were crossed out and next to them written, *Mrs. Watson,* and the letter continued.) — *we sorely need the help of Mr. Holmes, who I believe is the only man alive who can straighten out this mess. Ronnie has been locked up like a common criminal for nearly a week, and the police are unwilling to listen to his side of the story. They say the evidence is too strong against him.*

This was becoming worse and worse.

We do not have a lot of money, but I would gladly give everything we have to Mr. Holmes if he could extricate Ronnie out from under this horrible charge. He is innocent. Please, please, help us.

The girl's request was as clear as it was urgent; the problem was, I had absolutely no idea how to get in touch with Sherlock Holmes, or even where he was at present. It was possible that John knew, but John was on a train headed for the Highlands.

I rose and walked, somewhat unsteadily, over to John's writing desk and sat down. Taking up the pen and a sheet of paper, I began to compose a return missive to poor Bella stating that I was, alas, unable to help her. After struggling with the first paragraph, I was struck with an idea. So what if Sherlock Holmes was unobtainable? Did that mean the poor girl had nowhere else to turn?

Dared I actually attempt what I was contemplating? The part of me that had become so crushingly bored with sitting and looking out the window that I wanted to scream, was shouting *Yes!*

'Missy,' I called, 'could you come here for a moment?' The girl trotted in from the bedroom, feather duster in hand. 'Yes'm?' 'Please leave your duties for the time being and run to Waterloo Station to find out the train schedules.'

'Train schedules?'

'Yes, Missy. We are going to Bath.'

2

We boarded the train out of Paddington Station early the next morning.

While I had never been to Bath, I was more than familiar with Charles Dickens' treatment of it through *The Pickwick Papers*, my copy of which I had brought along to read on the train. The only distraction to my reading came from Missy, who *ooh*ed and *ahh*ed her way across the countryside, marvelling at every sight from a manor house to a cow. Before long the city was announced both by the cry of the conductor, a small, penguinish man with a surefooted rolling gate that seemed impervious to the motions of the train car, and a sign which proclaimed it 'Bath Spa'. As the train slowed, we gathered our things, and upon its stopping, made a sprint for the station platform.

Bath was set in a hollow surrounded by verdant hills, which were dotted with examples of the city's distinctive Georgian stone houses — each the colour of a well-circulated half-crown — and split by the river Avon. As we waited on the platform for our bags, I approached the stationmaster's window, which was manned by a fellow of such age and natural dust that I could not help wondering if he had been installed here along with the panelling in some earlier era.

'I have just arrived here, and my travelling companion and I will be staying for a few days,' I told the man. 'I am looking for a reasonably-priced hotel or boarding house. Do you happen to know of any?'

Scratching his bony chin, the stationmaster replied: 'You might want to try the Roman Hotel. It just opened up for visitors. The woman who runs it is Irish, but she can't help that, can she?'

After taking down the address and directions from the man, I collected Missy and strode to the front of the station, where a cab was conveniently waiting. Giving the address to the driver, a coarse looking fellow who loaded our luggage clumsily onto the brougham as though testing its sturdiness, we stepped inside and held on as the horse swiftly clopped down the narrow, circular road from the station and took us into the centre of town.

The Roman Hotel turned out to be decidedly un-Roman in appearance, though it looked inviting. It was quite large, built with the same golden-grey stone as the rest of the city, and sat atop a sloping, grassy yard that, frankly, could have used a bit more attention.

The driver of the cab leapt down and began to pull our luggage off, but I told him to wait. 'Leave everything where it is, if you will,' I said, stepping out of the cab. 'I have not yet determined whether there is indeed a room available, so you will stay here, with our luggage intact, until I have done so.'

Eight stone steps led up to the small porch, and there I rapped on the ornate front door that had an oval of glass in it. A moment later it was opened by a sturdy woman with a careworn face. Her black hair was fashionably pinned up, though a lock of it had escaped from her pompadour and fell over her left eye, creating the image of a question mark.

'Tis a room you're here about, then?' she asked, with a pronounced Irish accent.

'Yes, you were recommended by the stationmaster,' I said. 'I should like to see one of your rooms before making a decision as to whether my companion and I will stay here.'

'Of course, please come in.'

The house had a very comfortable looking day room off the main hallway and a smallish dining room opposite. The faint odour of paint permeated the interior, as befit an establishment that had only recently opened for business.

'All the rooms upstairs are to let,' the woman said, pushing the stray lock out of her face. 'I'm sure 'tis satisfied you'll be with any one of them.' She led me upstairs and showed the first of her available rooms, and while it did indeed look satisfactory, it was a bit small for two people. The second of the rooms seemed more suitable. It was cosy, but had two windows; and, best of all, two beds.

'How much are you asking?' I inquired, and she quoted me a price that sounded quite reasonable, albeit with that same tone of uncertainty, as though she felt like she was asking too much. 'Fine,' I said, smiling at her, 'we'll take it.'

'Wonderful!' she said, looking quite relieved. Then she caught herself, and in a more professional voice asked, 'How long will you be staying?'

'Two or three days, possibly longer.'

That seemed to please her no end. She led me back downstairs, all the while rattling off times for breakfast, the schedule for locking the front door, bath and laundry considerations, and other information that, while undoubtedly pertinent, came out so encumbered by the North Irish accent that I was not able to absorb half of it. What I did catch was that her name was Elizabeth Grimes. While she went to fetch the guest register, I repaired outside to instruct the cabman to bring the luggage in, which he did with all the solicitude of an ailing ox. When he was finished he accepted his fare with barely a 'thank you', leapt back into his seat, spurred his horse, and pulled away so quickly as to imply our patronage had made him tardy for some other engagement. I hope he was not representative of his trade in this city.

In the lobby Elizabeth Grimes presented the guestbook, and my suspicions were confirmed: Missy and I were the hotel's maiden guests. 'I hope we will be satisfactory roomers, Miss Grimes,' I said, signing the book.

'Actually it's *Mrs.* Grimes, though my husband is deceased.'

'Oh, I am sorry.'

'Killed in Africa, he was, three years ago, fighting the Boers.'

'At least it was in service of his country,' I said, hoping to be of some small comfort.

'Aye, *his* country,' she spat, and suddenly her accent took on new significance. Squinting at the book, she read: 'Mrs. Amelia Watson, and Missy ...'

'Trelawney,' I said. 'My maid.'

After leading us up the stairs to our room, Mrs. Grimes said, 'If there's anything you'll be needin', just holler. I'll be around someplace.'

After we had settled in the room, I announced to Missy that I was going into town.

'Do I need to dress up to go, mum?' she asked.

'Actually, dear, I would like you to stay here until I return.'

'What am I to do while you're gone?'

'I have brought something for you to read.' I opened my suitcase, withdrew a well-worn book and handed it to the girl.

She took it tentatively and examined the cover. 'North ... Northang ... '

'*Northanger Abbey*,' I finished for her. 'It is set partly in Bath, and I think you will enjoy it.'

'You won't ask me questions about it, will you?' she inquired grimly.

'I am no longer working as a governess, Missy. Besides, I have always felt that the best reading is voluntary reading, so I want you to voluntarily read that while I am gone.'

Going back downstairs, I found Mrs. Grimes watering a hanging plant in the day room. 'Yes, ma'am?' she said as soon as she saw me.

'I need to locate an address,' I said, producing the envelope that had come from Bella Standish. Mrs. Grimes took a look at it and gasped.

''Tis Ronald Standish the murderer you're lookin' for?'

'I am here to see the wife of Ronald

Standish, who has yet to be tried for any crime, and must therefore not yet be condemned.'

'He's murderer enough for the papers,' she said, and I began to see a little of the atmosphere of hopelessness and distress that Bella must be feeling. At that moment I realised I had better find out as much as I could about exactly what was being said about the killing. I asked if she happened to still have copies of the newspapers in question, and she disappeared into the back, returning a minute or so later with a stack of well-read papers. Thanking her, I took them to the sitting room.

According to the published accounts, a local businessman named George Frankham had engaged Ronald Standish to design and construct a patio garden for his home. After work on the project had started, a violent argument broke out between the two, apparently over the fact that young Standish's digging had covered far more of an area than Frankham had intended, thus destroying the entire yard. Several neighbours claimed to have witnessed or heard the argument, and while the details differed somewhat, the testimony of each agreed on one point: in the heat of anger, Ronald Standish had threatened to kill his employer.

There it might have rested if the body of George Frankham had not been discovered at the bottom of the Great Roman Bath in the middle of town, a mark on the back of his head proclaiming him the victim of a blow. A heavy wooden folding measuring tool, presumed to be the murder weapon, had been found nearby. Not only did the ruler bear the initials 'RS', but at the coroner's inquest Ronald Standish had actually identified it as his own, though claimed that he had lost it the day before Frankham's death. No one believed his story and young Standish was arrested.

It was easy to see why Bella had been so desperate to enlist Mr. Holmes' help in the case.

After obtaining directions to Albert Street from Mrs. Grimes (who crossed herself and bade that God go with me), I set out to find Bella Standish.

The day had a clearness and freshness to it that one rarely finds in London. The sky overhead was of a startling blue, and the sun, unobscured by cloud, fog, or tall buildings and spires on every street, was more powerful than I was used to. Even stranger to the ears of a Londoner was the relative quiet of the streets, which were not filled with the sounds of shouting newsvendors, street performers, yelling urchins or the combined neighing of a thousand horses who invariably complained as they battled their way through the city, carrying their charges. Life was definitely slower here.

In contrast to the almost uniform Georgian stone structures, Albert Street was lined with much more recently- (and modestly-) built wooden houses, each one tall and narrow, with planter boxes outside every front window. As I turned into the street, I saw that there was no need to follow the house numbers to find the home of the Standishes. It was surely the one that had a half-dozen men milling about the front, watched over by a portly, middle-aged constable. The men I took to be reporters, waiting for Bella Standish — or anyone else, for that matter — to come out; and the PC, I surmised, had been stationed there for the protection of anyone inside the house.

As soon as the men noticed me, they stopped pacing. When they realised that I was indeed headed for the Standish home, they became interested. I had no sooner set foot upon the walk in front of the house and turned to go up the steps, when they began shouting out questions. *Who are you? Are you a relative of Ronald Standish? Tell us why you're here! Give us your name, lady! Come on, ducky, say somethin'!*

All of this was drowned out by the constable bellowing, 'Come off, come off, all o' you!' Pushing them back, he approached me. 'Like a pack o' snappin' hounds,' he said, and I could see a genuine sense of disgust on his face. The constable introduced himself as PC Richter, and were he ever to retire from active duty, he could have applied for work in any Gilbert and Sullivan company in the world.

'Members of the press?' I asked.

'Aye. Most of those blokes are from neighboring towns. 'Correspondents', they call themselves. Royal pains, I call 'em. May I ask what you want with the Standish family?'

I presented the envelope as though it were a calling card. 'I was asked to come here by Bella — that is, Mrs. Standish. I am an old friend. Is there a problem with my going in?'

He looked at the envelope and handed it back. 'No ma'am, no problem at all. Go right ahead.'

'Thank you, officer.' The braying of the press resumed as I walked up the stairs and knocked on the door, but I ignored it, leaving it to the constable to re-establish peace and quiet. After several seconds there was no answer, so I knocked again. Then I heard a weary-sounding woman's voice on the other side ask: 'Who is it?'

'I am here to see Mrs. Standish,' I called through the door. 'My name is Amelia Watson.'

In a flash the door was pulled open and a petite young woman stood on the threshold, her mouth open in surprise. 'Miss Pettigrew!' Bella Standish cried. 'I mean, Mrs. Watson! I didn't expect you to come here in person.'

Had I seen her walking on the street, I would not have recognised Bella at all. As a child she had been full-faced and on the plump side, with long, lustrous hair, but now she was quite thin, with mouse-colored locks that fell skitter-scatter over her drawn, pale face. The only remnants of the old Bella were the large dark eyes, which seemed even larger given her present gauntness.

At the sight of Bella in the doorway, the reporters charged the staircase, shouting out questions as they battled for place. 'Come in, quickly,' she said, practically pulling me inside the house and slamming the door behind me. There were several poundings on the door before all fell quiet again.

'Good heavens, has it been like this the whole time?' I asked.

'Since Ronnie's arrest was first reported,' she said. 'I don't know how much more of it I can take. Oh, Miss Pettigrew, I am so glad you are here!' She threw herself into my arms and began to sob. I comforted her as best I could.

'Forgive me,' she said, finally releasing me and dabbing at her eyes. 'You must think me terribly rude. It's just that I am finding that what few manners I had before the ... incident are quickly deserting me.

Shall I make some tea?'

'That would be lovely, Bella, thank you.'

She led me into a comfortably-, if not luxuriously-, furnished day room, which would have been light and airy had the windows not been curtained. 'I cannot even uncover a window,' she explained, as I seated myself on a green settee. 'It's as though I were in prison myself, like poor Ronnie.' She looked up, her face suddenly illuminated. 'Is Mr. Holmes coming?'

I sighed. 'I am afraid not, dear. The truth is, I have no idea how to contact him.'

The poor girl sank to her knees. 'Then there is no hope.'

Rushing to her, I picked her up and walked her back into the day room and sat her down in a rather threadbare chair. 'Bella, there is always hope, and there are many problems in the world that manage to get resolved without the assistance of Sherlock Holmes. Perhaps I can be of assistance myself.'

'How? Have you become a detective?'

'Hardly, though one cannot be married to Dr. John Watson and have come into the company of Sherlock Holmes without picking up a rough idea of how the trick is done. I have, in my own small way, assisted the Metropolitan Police in London with the odd case or two.' I stopped short of telling her that I had actually assisted His Majesty King Edward with an odd case or two, for fear she would not believe me. There are days when I hardly believe it myself.

'Will you help Ronnie?' she asked, as needful as a child asking for shelter.

'I will certainly try,' I replied. 'Though it looks as though I must first help someone else.'

'Who is that?'

'You, Bella. When was the last time you sat down and ate a meal?'

'I don't know,' she said. 'The bread ran out yesterday and I cannot leave to get more.'

'Oh, heavens, child, this is not the way to steel yourself against an ordeal. You sit here and let me look around in your kitchen to see if there isn't something I can make for you.'

'Miss Pettigrew, really, you don't have to do this.'

'Clearly I do; and, please, I have not been

Miss Pettigrew for three years now. I am Mrs. Watson. Better yet, Amelia.'

'That may take some getting used to,' she said, giving me a wan smile.

Going to the small, dingy kitchen, I burrowed through a cupboard until I found a tin of beef, which I was able to make somewhat palatable, and brought it to her. She dove into it, as though suddenly realizing just how hungry she really was.

Once she had finished, I sat down and began to press her for details of her husband's situation.

'If you knew Ronnie, even for a short while, you would realise how utterly ridiculous these charges are,' she said. 'He could no more have killed that man than he can fly. His character does not possess the requisite violence.'

'According to the newspapers, his argument with this Mr. Frankham became rather menacing.'

'Men like George Frankham, who are born into wealth and position, hate men like Ronnie, who have to work for everything they have.'

'You may be right, Bella, but surely there

was more to the argument than societal snobbery. If I am to help, you must tell me everything. How did the argument start?'

She rose and began to pace the room in an agitated manner. 'It was all so foolish. Ronnie was levelling a small hillside behind Frankham's house, and as he dug he began to uncover some kind of ancient artefacts that were buried there. He considered them lost treasure. Ronnie has a passion for archaeology; that is one of the reasons we are living in Bath, because there is so much ancient history around here. The more he dug, the more of these things he found. You would have to ask him what they are. But after a while he forgot all about the patio.'

'That would explain Mr. Frankham's anger. When he saw how little work was being done on the patio, he must have exploded, just as the newspaper accounts have it.'

Bella stopped pacing. 'But the newspapers are wrong! This is what I've tried to tell the police. Frankham wasn't angry at all! Not then, anyway. When Ronnie showed Frankham the things he had found, he said the man became as excited about them as he had. He actually told Ronnie to abandon the patio project and make it a real excavation site, which he did.'

The girl resumed pacing. 'The argument came later. It was over what to do with the artefacts. Frankham tried to take them away from Ronnie, saying they were for his private collection, since they had been found on his property. Ronnie felt they should be studied by experts and put in museums. At one point Frankham accused Ronnie of stealing the artefacts. He said that he wasn't paying Ronnie to dig up his property and then keep the buried treasure like some pirate. That is the part that the witnesses overheard. That's why the newspapers reported that Frankham was angry that Ronnie had dug up his yard without permission. But it isn't true.'

'So the only thing that made Mr. Frankham angry was the fact that Ronnie didn't want to give him the artefacts?'

Bella nodded.

'And where are these artefacts now?'

'Frankham has most of them. He threw Ronnie off his property and kept everything ... everything except this.'

She walked over to a desk, opened the drawer, and pulled something out from under a stack of papers. Carrying it back, she dropped it in my hand. It was a medallion of some kind, roughly the diameter of a teacup, and obviously very old. Its fragile chain was encrusted in centuries' worth of dirt, though the disc of the medallion had been cleaned, revealing what looked like bronze at first, but upon closer inspection, turned out to be gold.

I held it under a lamp to get a better look, and in the light a face could be seen, though whether it was supposed to be a human face I was unable to say. It was round and had a widely opened mouth surrounded by a thick moustache and beard. Despite the beard, the face had a distinctly fish-like quality. There was a sunburst pattern around the head, which might have been hair, or it might have been part of a decorative background. Most distinctive of all, however, were the eyes, which were wide open and staring, as though looking straight at me, an effect that was quite disconcerting.

'Ronnie secreted this away from the site?'

I asked.

'Yes. He managed to slip it into the pocket of his cloth apron in which he usually carried his measuring tool — which is why he left the tool behind, the tool the police think he used to kill Frankham.'

'Wait a minute, Bella. The papers said Ronnie claimed he didn't know where or how he lost the ruler.'

'He had to say that. He couldn't tell the police he left it behind to make room in his pocket for the precious artefact he was taking with him. That would have made things so much worse.'

As I sat thinking about what she had told me and how it fit in with the evidence the police had, I began to wonder if it was even possible for things to get any worse than they already were for Ronnie Standish.

3

Having done my best to assure Bella that there was nothing to worry about, that Ronnie would eventually be cleared — perhaps my finest performance since my youthful days with the Laurence Delancey Amateur Players — I left her feeling somewhat at ease. If only it were so.

Outside, I once more braved the crowd of reporters long enough to ask PC Richter for directions to the nearest grocer's shop, informing him of my plan to arrange for fresh food to be delivered to the house.

'Aye, ma'am, I'll see that it gets inside,' he promised.

Fortunately, the grocer's was quite close, and the owner was more than happy to accommodate my wishes (then again, I was careful not to mention the name Standish, but merely gave him the address). Once my business there was complete, I returned to the Roman Hotel.

Giving a quick rap on the door of our

room, I announced, 'It is I, Missy,' and walked in, only to find the room deserted. My copy of *Northanger Abbey* lay closed on the bed. Surely the girl had not gone out on her own, after I had specifically requested that she wait here for me.

I started back down the stairs to ask Mrs. Grimes if she happened to have seen her, but halfway to the first floor, my question became redundant. From my vantage point on the stairs I could see into the house's dining room, and there was Missy, a feather duster tucked into her belt, putting fresh flowers into a vase that sat atop a mahogany bureau. As I stepped into the room, she noticed me.

'Oh, hello, mum,' she said. 'I didn't have nothing to do, so I offered to help Mrs. Grimes out.'

"I didn't have *anything* to do', Missy,' I corrected.

'Oh, I thought you did, mum.'

From the next room, Mrs. Grimes called out: 'When you're done with that, lovie, the dishes could use a good wipe.'

'Missy, what about the book I gave to you?' I asked.

The girl made a face. 'Cleaning's more interesting than that was, mum.'

'I see.' Turning into the direction from which I had heard the landlady's voice, I called: 'Mrs. Grimes, might I speak with you?'

'Ooh, 'tis back ye are!' she cried, practically running into the dining room, wiping her hands on her apron, her face stretched into a broad smile. She took my hand. 'Now, why didn't you tell me you were the wife of Dr. Watson of Baker Street?'

I cast my eyes over at the maid, who had finished with the flowers and was now feathering away some dust, real or imagined. 'Have you been tattling, Missy?' I asked.

'I was only talking about the doctor, mum,' she replied. 'You know, what he was like to work for and all, and it turned out that Mrs. Grimes had some of his books.'

'I don't suppose he'll be joinin' you here, will he?' the landlady asked.

'He has a pressing engagement elsewhere, though I am sure he will be delighted to know that we stayed at the home of a devoted reader. Mrs. Grimes, about Missy —'

'Oh, a godsend she is!' the woman cried. ''Tis hard to keep the place up all by my lonesome, and when the girl offered to help, why, I couldn't believe my good fortune.'

'Yes, Missy's a jewel,' I agreed, half-heartedly, 'although when I took the room here, it was under the assumption that we would be guests at this house, not workers.'

'I don't mind, mum, really,' Missy chimed in; and looking over, I could see the ease and contentment on her face as she went about her cleaning and straightening.

I sighed. If I had thought that the girl was going to take advantage of this visit to improve her mind by reading, or by visiting the historical buildings and sites, I was clearly in error. 'Very well, Missy, you may offer your services whenever you have the time, though please do not forget that I may need to call upon you as well.'

'Yes'm,' she responded, going back to her dusting, while Mrs. Grimes disappeared into the back.

Halfway up the stairs, an idea struck me. Turning back, I said: 'When you are done with that, Missy, would you come to the sitting room for a moment?'

'Yes'm,' she replied, as I stole into the room and waited for her on the small couch. She came in a minute later. 'You're not cross about me helping the missus out, are you?'

'It's fine, dear, but I have another task for you.'

'Is it hard?'

'Not at all. In fact, it will be doing exactly what you do at home for me and are now doing for Mrs. Grimes, but instead you will be doing it for Mrs. Standish.'

'Taking care of her house?'

'Exactly. Bella — Mrs. Standish — has been rather distracted of late, and the house shows it. Since you are here and so eager to work, you would be helping everyone by giving her a hand. I will explain everything to Mrs. Grimes, so you need not worry about leaving her.'

'All right, mum.'

'Good. Go fetch your bag and we shall go straight over.'

'You mean I'll be staying there?'

'For the time being. Now go, dear.'

Missy's expression indicated that she thought there was something behind my request, and she was quite right. Certainly Bella's home did need cleaning and straightening, and constant companionship would do her good as well. What I did not tell Missy, however, was that while there, she would be in essence a kind of spy for me, one who would report on anything and everything Bella might say, and who her visitors were. It would, in short, provide me with eyes and ears inside the house while enabling me to pursue an investigation of things elsewhere.

After all, wasn't this exactly what Mr. Holmes had done with my husband in that bizarre case of the starved dog that was turned loose on the Baskerville heir?

Mrs. Grimes reappeared in the lobby just in time to see Missy descending the stairs, suitcase in hand. ''Tis not leaving ye are!' she cried, looking rather alarmed.

'Mrs. Grimes, I'm afraid I have to take Missy away from here for the time being,' I told her. 'However, I shall remain, and in time, Missy will return as well.'

Even though the landlady looked disappointed at this turn of events, there was little she could do but accept it. 'Come along, Missy,' I said, taking the girl by the arm and hastening down the street out of the hotel. Given Missy's luggage and my concern about overtaxing my ankle by walking, I decided to hail a cab.

As we approached the house in Albert Street I could see that a few of the reporters had left, though PC Richter remained at his post. 'Back so soon, ma'am?' he asked as I climbed out of the cab.

'I suppose you could say I forgot something,' I replied.

The reporters began to swirl around Missy and me, but the constable kept them at bay. 'The food box you were talking about came a few minutes ago,' he said. 'Mr. Creach took it in.'

'Mr. Creach?'

'The lawyer.'

Ignoring the din of the reporters, who were shouting: *Come on, lady, tell us who you are!* and *You the girl's mum?* and *You think the husband did it?*, I knocked on the door of the house, and it was quickly opened by a man. He was youngish and nattily dressed in a dark grey suit with matching waistcoat and a burgundy cravat held fast by a pearl stickpin. His dark hair was expertly barbered and oiled in place. While not particularly large, he was standing in the doorway in such a way as to effectively block my entry of it.

'You must be Mr. Creach,' I said. 'I am Amelia Watson, and I am here to see Mrs. Standish.'

'Ah, Mrs. Watson,' the man replied familiarly, and stepped aside. 'Do come in. Bella told me you had arrived. I am Geoffrey Creach, esquire.'

'How do you do?' I said, breezing past him and pulling Missy along with me. 'Bella, I have brought along my maid, Missy. Perhaps she can help you around the house for the time that we are in the city.'

'Oh, Miss Pet — I mean, Amelia — I can't let you do that.'

'Nonsense, Missy loves housework.'

Having fully taken in the condition of Bella's house, which was far more in need of a good cleaning than the Roman Hotel, Missy smiled wanly.

'Thank you,' Bella said, suddenly tearful. 'Everybody is being so good to me, I don't know what to say. Mr. Creach has agreed to act as our solicitor, even though he knows our financial situation.'

'Now, now, Bella, enough of that,' the lawyer said gently.

'How do you rate Ronnie's predicament, Mr. Creach?' I asked.

'If I may be permitted an analogy, Mrs. Watson,' he replied, 'this case will be like circling the running track at Eton: exhausting, perhaps even punishing, but ultimately we will finish victorious.'

'But will Ronnie be able to keep his winner's medallion?' I went on, rather pointedly, while studying the man closely.

'Hmm? Oh, you mean, will he win the metaphorical race and be set free? Unquestioningly,' Mr. Creach answered.

That was, of course, not what I had meant. I was testing him to see, without asking in so many words, whether he knew about the medallion that Ronnie had found and was keeping secret from the police, and Mr. Creach provided no indication whatever that he did. So Bella and Ronnie were withholding this important bit of information even from their legal counsel. This did not bode well.

I turned back to Missy and instructed her to carry out Bella Standish's wishes as though they were mine, and watched as Bella took the girl back into the kitchen. When I was alone in the day room with Mr. Creach, he leaned in closely. 'May I speak to you privately, Mrs. Watson?' he asked.

'Very well,' I replied.

Peering over my shoulder to make sure Bella was not watching or listening, he then led me further into the room, next to the simple fireplace. Speaking in a very low voice, he said: 'I understand that you are an acquaintance of Sherlock Holmes, and that your husband is the doctor whom he has befriended, is that so?'

'It is.'

'You realise, of course, that Bella carries the hope of engaging the detective to investigate this case.'

'That is why she contacted me, Mr. Creach, though I had to deliver the news to her that Mr. Holmes is unavailable.'

'That is very good news.'

While I admit I have not always considered the presence of Sherlock Holmes to be beneficial, I was puzzled as to why this young attorney was so against his becoming involved. 'How is it good news?'

'The truth is, Mrs. Watson, I feel involving Sherlock Holmes in this matter would do more harm to my client than good. You have seen the wolf pack out there. The member of the press, waiting for any bone, no matter small, on which to make an entire public meal. If they were to learn that the great Sherlock Holmes was working on behalf of Ronnie Standish, this entire case would be turned into a circus, and should that happen, Standish is all but lost.'

'How so?'

'Because justice is not comfortable riding an elephant or swinging from a trapeze. When the trappings of a case become the main focus, the heart of the case, the guilt or innocence of a man, becomes dwarfed by the spectacle. The audience begins to demand not a mere resolution to a trial, but a grand finale, an ending that is commensurate with all that has preceded it. Ronald Standish must be the star of his own trial, not Sherlock Holmes.'

Even though the argument as presented by Geoffrey Creach was steeped in melodrama, I could see his point.

Bella chose that moment to return from the kitchen. 'Thank you, Amelia,' she said. 'You have no idea how much having Missy here is going to help me.'

'I am glad to be of help,' I replied. 'I was wondering, Bella, if I might be able to see Ronnie and talk to him.'

Bella opened her mouth to answer, but before she could say anything, Geoffrey Creach declared: 'Oh, I think not, Mrs. Watson. I mean, to what end? We are all grateful for the help you have already provided to dear Bella, but there is no reason I can think of why you should wish to visit a cold, uninviting gaol and speak to the unfortunate prisoner.'

'So you are forbidding it?'

"Forbid' is such a harsh word,' he said smoothly. 'Let us say that, in my capacity as Mr. Standish's solicitor, I do not see the advantage to it.'

'But I would like Amelia to speak with Ronnie,' Bella said.

'I cannot see what it could hurt,' I added.

Geoffrey Creach seemed to realise that he had lost the argument. 'Very well, if you insist. I will take her there myself, though I do so under protest.' From a table he picked up a felt hat the colour of his suit, and a walking stick. 'We can leave right away if you have no other plans, Mrs. Watson.'

'I do not,' I replied, heading towards the front door.

'Not that way,' Mr. Creach said. 'We must leave the premises through the back.'

'Through the back?' Bella said. 'But the walkway in the yard will only take you around the side of the house and past the front anyway. If your desire is to escape the notice of the press, that will not help.'

'This all seems rather mysterious, Mr. Creach,' I confessed.

'I ask that you trust me, Mrs. Watson. And do not worry, Bella, we shall be able to slip past the gentlemen at the front door. This way, then, Mrs. Watson.'

I followed the solicitor through the back door into the small, square yard behind the Standish home, and immediately I realised what Bella had been talking about regarding the escape route. The yard was surrounded on three sides by a shoulder-high brick wall, the only opening of which led to a narrow pavement that clearly ran past the side of the house and back out through the front.

'Mr. Creach, unless you have managed to construct a tunnel underneath that wall, it would appear that we are trapped,' I commented.

'Not at all,' he said, walking to the wall at the rear of the yard. Setting his walking stick atop it, he placed his gloved hands beside it and, in one deft movement, sprung atop it and stayed there, crouched, careful not to let any part of his clothing touch the rough brick. 'Come, I shall help you.'

'You have got to be joking,' I said, coolly.

'It is the only way, Mrs. Watson.'

Immediately, I thought of my ankle; the last thing I needed was the further injury of my foot while attempting to clamber over the back wall of a former pupil's house like some kind of she-ape recently escaped from the zoo. 'I am sorry, Mr. Creach, but this is quite out of the question. I will not behave like a daylight burglar, not for you or anyone.'

The solicitor sighed. 'I understand madam, and I apologise. I should not have expected so much from a woman.'

At those words, I bristled. For more than sixty years a woman sat on the throne of England, a time when the Empire was strengthened and respected as never before, and in three short years under male rule it is rare to find a man anywhere on the island willing to credit a woman with enough native intelligence and resourcefulness to tie her own bootlaces! My indignation must have been registering on my face, for Mr. Creach inquired: 'Have I said something that distressed you, madam?'

'Only your implication that women are lesser forms of humanity by virtue of our gender.'

'I beg your pardon?'

'You were quite right, Mr. Creach, in that it was ridiculous to ask me to clamber over a brick wall, given that I endeavour to comport myself with an air of refinement at all times, but please do not make the mistake of assuming that I am unable to execute such a feat simply because I am a woman.'

'The furthest thought from my mind,' he replied, glibly.

Did I detect a note of sarcasm in his voice? 'You do not believe me?' I challenged.

'Mrs. Watson, I said nothing of the sort.'

'Stand aside, Mr. Creach,' I commanded, looking about the yard for a crate, a box, or even a large stone. My eye finally lit upon the base of a baked-clay birdbath, which was half-hidden under a tree near the corner of the yard. I marched to it and picked it up, and upon discovering it to be quite light, carried it over to the wall and set it down firmly a few inches away from the brick. Still crouching atop the wall, Geoffrey Creach offered a hand, which I politely refused. 'No thank you, I can manage,' I said, placing both hands on the top of the wall, and my non-weakened foot on top of the birdbath base, lifting myself up until I was seated on top of the bricks.

'Well done, Mrs. Watson,' Mr. Creach said, leaping off the other side.

I swung my legs around, victorious, and — still mindful of potential injury to my ankle — this time accepted his assistance in lowering myself to the ground. And that was that.

We were now in an alleyway, which, Mr. Creach assured me, was empty. 'No one here to hear us,' he said, leading me out to the side-street with no one from the press pack the wiser.

'You say you have used this escape route before?' I asked.

'A time or two,' he replied.

'And none of the reporters stationed in front of Bella Standish's home wonders why you enter the house through the front door, but never return?'

He stopped and regarded me, his clear blue eyes brightly reflecting the sunlight. 'An astute observation, madam. I imagine I have gotten away with it because old Richter clears the crowd periodically, shooing them away, so that no one person keeps his vigil for more than a few hours, so they are not there to see whether I emerge or not. And Richter, I have discovered, is not the most observant of souls. But now that you have brought this to my attention, I see that I must take special precaution so as not to plant an untoward note of suspicion. Thank you for pointing it out to me.'

As we walked to the street, the solicitor raised his walking stick to flag down a hansom. 'Before we drop in on Ronnie,' he said, 'you should see the Roman Bath.'

'I am not really here as a tourist, Mr. Creach,' I said.

'Do not think of it as a tourist destination, then. Think of it as the scene of the crime.'

That was different. More to the point, however, I was at the moment in Geoffrey Creach's power, since I doubted I would be able to get into the local gaol to see Ronnie Standish on my own. If my host decided to visit Stonehenge as a pre-requirement, there was not much I could do about it.

I could, however, remain inquisitive.

Once we were inside the cab and on our way, I said: 'Do you mind, Mr. Creach, if I ask a personal question?'

'The name of my tailor?'

'No, the fact that you are taking on Ronnie's case without the expectation of payment.'

He smiled. 'That puzzles you, does it?'

'I must confess that it does, a bit. I cannot help but presume that there is still something you hope to gain personally from your efforts on his behalf.'

'How old do you think I am, Mrs. Watson?'

'How old?' I repeated, somewhat taken aback by the unexpected question. 'I don't know: thirty-five, perhaps?'

'I am thirty-eight. Hardly a callow youth. However, many of my peers at the bar, as fusty a collection of old Sirs as ever hobbled the realm, regard me as little better than an apprentice, and a foolhardy one for even thinking that there is no such thing as a case with a foregone conclusion. I have become involved as a way of proving them wrong about the case, about Standish, and about me.'

'I see. How do you really rate Ronnie's chances?'

'In terms of the so-called evidence, there is nothing the prosecution can offer that I cannot put into question. That argument between Standish and Frankham, for example, was simply that and nothing more. As for the alleged murder weapon, the only way to know for certain that it is even possible to kill a man with a folded wooden ruler is to attempt it, and I daresay that the King's Court is not going to allow such an experiment.'

'You are confident, then, that Ronnie will

be acquitted?'

His face turned serious. 'There is only one area of vulnerability in this case, Mrs. Watson, one question that I at present cannot answer, but which the prosecution will make much of for their own gain.'

'What is that?'

'If Ronald Standish did not kill George Frankham, who did? And for what reason?'

We spoke no more until we arrived at the Great Bath, which was accessed through a building called the Pump Room.

Standing on the stone terrace that overlooked it, I admit that I was not quite prepared for the ancient majesty of its well-preserved remains, evidence of a long-dead civilisation that rested comfortably in the shadow of the vast abbey. Like so much of England, the only new elements were the people, who would all come and go, and live and die, while these edifices remained, century after century.

Geoffrey Creach walked to one corner of the stone rail.

'The police believe that Frankham must have fallen from here,' he said. There is nothing upon which he could have hit his head below, which is why the investigating officer is certain that he was attacked before he fell — or was pushed — into the bath.'

'Surely this could not have taken place in broad daylight,' I said, 'so what on earth was Mr. Frankham doing here at night?'

'That is something that no one can answer — save, perhaps, the murderer.'

'How do you suppose he even got up here?'

'I beg your pardon?'

'This terrace is several feet above the street level. We came through that building ... what did you call it?'

'The Pump Room.'

'Yes, but is the Pump Room open at night for access to the Bath? If not, how did he get up here?'

'He could have used a ladder, I suppose.'

'A man does not carry a ladder through the streets, while the town sleeps around him, in order to climb up onto a secluded place and be murdered. That is the stuff of bad fiction, Mr. Creach.'

'Point taken,' he said, peering over the rail to the street below. 'I suppose it would be possible to climb up. We scaled a wall this very day, after all.'

'Please don't remind me. I will accept the argument that he climbed up, but that leaves another question: why? My experience with people has been that they rarely do things without reason, and never do unusual things without reason. If you can discover why Mr. Frankham was up here in the first place, I believe you will find the direction in which to look for the murderer.'

The dark-green, murky waters were not about to offer us any answers, so we exited back through the Pump Room and returned once more into the courtyard of the abbey, where a young man in a high-buttoned Georgian waistcoat and a rather yellowed-looking powdered wig was playing a pennywhistle for, well, pennies.I reached into my handbag and withdrew a tuppence, which I placed in the bowl that was set in front of him. He responded with a nod and a glissando, then returned once more to the tune he was playing, which I believe was a theme from Mozart.

'Mrs. Watson, you have just publicly proclaimed your status as a tourist,' Mr.

Creach said, smiling.

'I try to support the arts whenever possible,' I replied.

'Perhaps we should take in more of the city's sights.'

'Perhaps I am starting to be persuaded that you are deliberately trying to keep me away from seeing Ronnie.'

The solicitor did not deny it; he merely sighed.

'I shall tell you what,' I went on. 'You may take me to one more place before we visit the gaol. I wish to see the home of the late Mr. Frankham.'

'Frankham's house? Whatever for?'

'I shall tell you when we get there.'

The solicitor hailed another cab to take us to Ashdown Crescent, a stone semicircle of houses on the northern part of the city.

'There,' he said, pointing with his stick to a three-storey townhouse on the end of the crescent. 'That one was Frankham's house. The patio that Standish was working on is behind it, abutting the green. I suppose you would you like to see it, too?'

'If it is not too much trouble,' I replied.

Stepping out of the cab, Mr. Creach told

the driver to wait for us, and then escorted me behind the crescent where, in truth, there was very little to see due to a temporary wall that had been erected around the property.

'Feel free to take a look,' the solicitor said. 'There is a door in the wall, but please be careful.'

Stepping to the wall, which was some seven feet in height, I was able to find the door and cautiously peered inside. The ground had been thoroughly excavated, and the patch closest to the house was marked off by a series of stakes with thin rope strung between them.

'Satisfied, I trust?' Mr. Creach said behind me. 'Now will you tell me for what, exactly, you are looking?'

'Vision lines,' I told him.

'I beg your pardon?'

'Was this fence here at the time of the argument between Ronnie and Mr. Frankham?'

'I believe so.'

'And can the excavated area be seen from the windows of any of the surrounding houses?'

Geoffrey Creach looked at me curiously. 'I have no idea. Why do you ask?'

'It is just that the case against Ronnie weighs so heavily on that argument he had with Mr. Frankham; yet, unless one is able to see down from the windows of an adjoining house, it would be nearly impossible to have actually witnessed the argument.'

'I believe the witnesses stated that they *heard* the argument.'

'Then I remain puzzled. In any argument between men, it is more difficult to distinguish one voice from the other because the voices are raised and therefore distorted. Without the ability to see the two men, because of this wall, how could the witnesses be certain that it was Ronnie who made the threat? What if it was Mr. Frankham who made the threat? For that matter, if they could not see the two men in question, how can they be absolutely certain that it was Ronnie arguing with Mr. Frankham, and not somebody else?'

'I'm afraid it was indeed Standish, Mrs. Watson. He has admitted to having the argument. But the existence of this wall does indeed throw questions upon the credibility of the witnesses. You fairly amaze me, madam. Providing, of course, that I can prove this wall was indeed standing at the time of the argument.'

'There is one man who would know,' I said, sweetly. 'Why don't we ask him?'

Mr. Creach lowered his head and smiled. 'Very well, Mrs. Watson. We will go and see Standish in the gaol.'

We had travelled for several minutes in the cab when the journey began to take on a note of familiarity, even for a city in which so many buildings were identical. I realised that we were headed for the railway station. Was the solicitor attempting to rid himself of me by putting me on the next train? It was then that Mr. Creach explained that the city gaol was peculiarly located underneath the supports of the station. As we approached it, though, I could see a flurry of uniformed constables racing about, blowing whistles, running thither and yon as though in a great state of confusion.

'Somethin''s happenin', guv,' the cabman called down, though we could see that clearly enough for ourselves.

From outside a voice called 'Halt!' and

the face of a policeman appeared at the cab window. 'You can't go any further than this,' he said.

'What's happened?' Mr. Creach asked.

'Nothing that needs to concern you, sir. Driver, turn this thing around and go back where you came from.'

'Wait a minute. Constable, I am Geoffrey Creach, esquire, and I need to see a client of mine, Ronald Standish, who is being held in the gaol.'

'Did you say Standish?'

'Yes, Ronald Standish.'

The policeman puffed out his moustache. 'Well then, sir, I suppose it does concern you. I think the inspector would like to have a word with you.'

'What for?'

'It seems that Standish has escaped.'

4

It was I who chose to come here, I kept telling myself, as I waited uncomfortably in the small police station while Inspector James McCallum of the Bath constabulary did a very convincing imitation of a hurricane. *Nobody forced me to endure this.* At least I was outside the inspector's office, listening through the transom. It was Geoffrey Creach who was behind the closed door, bearing the brunt of the storm.

When the shouting had subsided, the door suddenly swung open and the inspector emerged. James McCallum was a compact, red-faced man almost as thick as he was tall, with a cannonball-shaped head that was perched squarely on his wide shoulders, somewhat resembling a round boulder atop a block.

'If you're still here in two minutes time, I'll bloody well throw you in the gaol to take Standish's place!' he shouted as he stormed down the hall of the station. He had taken no notice of me whatsoever. I might as well have been invisible.

Mr. Creach then stepped out of the office. 'It appears the inspector is a shade upset,' he said with remarkable understatement. Still, he wasted no time leaving the gaol.

Once we were outside, I said: 'I would hate to have been on the receiving end of that man's wrath.'

'I suspect his anger is really focused on his force who let Standish slip away,' Mr. Creach said, flagging yet another cab. 'I just happened to be a handy whipping boy.'

'I am glad you're not taking it personally.'

'Don't mistake me, Mrs. Watson. I believe our inspector to be a splendid example of the missing link. I just strive not to show any distress at his actions — which, of course, makes him even more irate.'

The cab arrived, a brougham this time, and Mr. Creach directed it to Albert Street. 'I hope we are in time to catch our escapee,' he said as we climbed in.

'You mean you expect Ronnie to go straight to his house?'

'Where else would he go?'

'But surely he knows that will be the first place the police look for him.'

The solicitor suddenly dropped his veneer of nonchalance. 'I don't know what he knows or what he doesn't know, Mrs. Watson. All I can say for certain is that McCallum will take his disappearance as a conclusive statement of his guilt. The only thing Standish could have done that is more incriminating as far as the police are concerned is to have written a confession in blood.'

I nodded. It did not look good for Ronnie Standish.

The cab rounded the corner to Albert Street, and immediately Mr. Creach sighed heavily. 'Just what I feared,' he muttered. Looking out of the window, I saw the cause of his trepidation. A platoon of police constables had already arrived and had built a human wall across the door of the Standishes' home, while the pack of reporters swarmed all around them like so many angry bees being kept from their honey. Knocking on the top of the cab with his stick, Mr. Creach called to the driver, 'Take us around to the back.'

73

'Not the wall again,' I groaned.

'I'm afraid we have no choice.'

The driver pulled past the crowd and turned into the first cross-street. 'Stop here,' Mr. Creach instructed the driver. Turning to me, he added: 'I'll make certain no one is in the back. When you hear my signal, follow me.' Then, sliding out of the cab, he flipped a coin up to the driver, dashed to the stone fence, and vaulted over it.

A few seconds later I heard his whistle and went up to the fence, managing to scale it for the second — and, as far as I was concerned, the last — time. Mr. Creach was rapping on the back door, which Missy finally opened. As we dashed in, Mr. Creach demanded, 'Where is Bella?'

'In the bedroom, lying down,' Missy replied.

'Upstairs?'

'Yes sir.'

'I'll go and check on her,' I said.

Trotting up the staircase I called: 'Bella, are you all right?' and heard a muffled whimper coming from behind a nearly-closed door to the right of the top landing. I called again — 'May I come in?' — and received permission. Inside the small but comfortable-looking room, Bella was stretched out on her bed, and her face showed signs that she had been crying. I went over and sat down on the edge of the bed.

'What do they want from me?' she moaned. 'All those people outside, why are they bothering us? Is there nothing else happening in this part of the country? I tried to go out earlier, just for a minute, just to see the sun, and I was nearly attacked. Even the police were unable to hold them back.' She began to sob. 'Why won't they go away?'

I tried to comfort her as best I could, but also realised that it was probably beneficial for her to get it all out of her system, and so let her continue sobbing before saying: 'Their job is to gather the news, and you are news. While I agree that they are a bit over-zealous in their manner, particularly in light of Ronnie's —' I stopped talking, knowing that this was no way to break the news to the girl that her husband had escaped.

Bella sat up and dabbed her eyes with a well-used handkerchief. 'In light of Ronnie's *what?*' she asked.

'Bella, I need you to answer me truthfully. Is Ronnie hiding in this house?'

'How could he be? You know he is being held at the gaol. I thought you were going to see him.'

'I was, Bella, but he escaped before we got there.'

She stared back at me with an expression that was equal parts confusion, shock and alarm. It was a look of such honest emotion that if she were merely pretending to be surprised at my news, she would have to be a finer actress than any I worked with in my youth, or have subsequently seen on the stage. 'Escaped?' she muttered. 'How?'

'I do not know,' I replied.

At that moment I heard a call from downstairs: 'Is there a problem, Mrs. Watson?'

'Pardon me, dear,' I said, stepping out of the bedroom to the landing. 'No, Bella is fine, though a bit stunned,' I called back. 'Would you like me to bring her down?'

'Yes, please, Mrs. Watson,' the solicitor replied.

I returned to the bedroom and found that Bella had already got out of bed. No longer sobbing, she now had the look of someone who was desperately trying to adjust to a great shock.

'Mr. Creach wishes to speak with you downstairs, Bella.'

'Yes, of course,' she said numbly.

She had descended only halfway down the stairs when Mr. Creach rushed up to her and demanded: 'Bella, have you seen Ronnie? Did he come here?'

I answered for the girl: 'I have already asked her, and I am satisfied that the answer is no. If he had come, I am certain Missy would have seen him as well.'

Mr. Creach spun around and placed his hands to his head, as though attempting to push away a great headache. 'This could ruin everything,' he muttered.

'How did Ronnie escape?' Bella asked.

'The story I received from McCallum, in between his incoherent screams, is that Ronnie was becoming agitated, pacing like an animal in a cage.'

'What did they expect?' Bella asked, shakily. 'They are *treating* him like an animal in a cage!'

'Just so, but apparently he became agitated to the point of panic, and one of the officers opened the cell to try and 'calm him down' — restrain him, more than likely. But Ronnie charged the man, knocked him to the floor, and dashed out of the cell. He continued to run, knocking aside anyone and everyone who attempted to stop him, until he had made it outside. That was the last anyone has seen of him.'

Bella sank into a nearby chair. 'I think I know what happened to him,' she went on. 'Last year he was digging on a hillside, looking for artefacts. He had dug a hole about the size of a grave and was standing at the bottom of it when suddenly one of the walls collapsed. Before he could get out, the dirt fell in on him like an avalanche, trapping him for more than an hour. A passer-by happened to hear his cries and, with the help of a few others, rescued him. He was unharmed, but frightened. The incident led him to learn a safer way to excavate, though it also left him with a dread fear of confinement. The truth is, had he not managed to escape, he might have become unhinged.'

'Well, that would explain it,' Mr. Creach mumbled. 'And you are certain you have no idea where Ronnie is?'

'None.'

'With the gaol so close to the train station, is it possible that he might try to board a train and leave the city entirely?' I asked.

'He would not leave without telling me,' Bella replied.

'Besides,' Mr. Creach added, 'one has to have money to buy a train ticket, and it is standard practice to remove all of a prisoner's possessions before incarcerating him.'

'I wish you would not use words such as those,' Bella begged. 'Ronnie is not a prisoner. He is innocent.'

'Yes, he is innocent, Bella,' the solicitor responded, 'but technically, anyone held in custody by the police is to be considered their prisoner.'

'I feel like a prisoner myself!' Bella declared. 'This house, the police, the reporters; they are all bearing down on me!'

'Reporters bear down on people?' Missy piped up. 'Is that why they're called the press?'

All of us turned towards Missy, who faced each of us with a growing sense of puzzlement. 'Did I say something wrong?' she asked. I was the first to begin laughing, followed by Mr. Creach, who tried to hide his smile behind his hand, and lastly Bella, who managed to transform her growing hysteria into laughter.

'Won't someone tell me what's so funny?' Missy asked again.

'Later, dear,' I said, and watched her shuffle back, puzzled, into the kitchen.

'Oh, I shouldn't be laughing,' Bella said, unable to stop. 'Not now, not with all the trouble Ronnie is in.'

'Ronnie will be in no less or no more trouble because of your laughter,' I said. 'It is permissible to allow yourself to be human.'

All of our smiles and laughter were put to an end a moment later, however, with the fierce pounding on the front door of the Standish home. 'Who is that?' Bella asked, startled by the sudden noise.

'I believe I know,' Mr. Creach said, moving towards the door. Even before he got there, we could hear the harsh voice shouting: 'Open up! Police business!' All traces of her earlier mirth having disappeared, Bella now looked pale and terrified, and leaned against a table for support. 'When is this going to end?' she moaned. I could only imagine what the poor girl was going through.

'I will deal with him,' Mr. Creach said. 'Sit down, Bella, and say as little as possible.'

Another pounding came, and Mr. Creach quickly opened the door to reveal Inspector McCallum. 'All right,' he spat, marching inside, 'where is he?'

'Where is who, Inspector?' Mr. Creach said, the soul of innocence.

'Standish, as if you didn't know.'

'He is not here,' I said.

Inspector McCallum turned to me and glowered. 'And who are you?'

'This is Mrs. Amelia Watson, McCallum, a friend of the Standish family,' Mr. Creach said. 'She was down at the station not a half-hour ago, along with me. I'm surprised you did not see her there.'

'I can't keep track of every stranger that comes into town!' he shouted. 'Well, Mrs. Amelia Watson, you picked a bloody poor time for a visit. But since you're here, I'll thank you to stay out of the way.'

In my dealings with the police of London,

I had encountered some with the churlish manner of Inspector McCallum; though very few, I am happy to say. They, however, did not intimidate me, and I had no intention of being intimidated by this brute. 'I am pleased to meet you as well,' I said, icily. 'But I reiterate that you are wasting your time. Ronnie is not here.'

'We'll see to that.' The inspector motioned through the door and three uniformed policemen dutifully entered the house. 'I want this place searched from top to bottom,' he ordered. 'You,' he said, pointing to one of them, 'look upstairs.' To the next one he barked: 'You check the back.' Turning to Bella, he demanded: 'Is there a cellar in this house?'

'Yes,' she whispered. 'The door is under the stairs.'

'Right,' the inspector said, jabbing a finger at the remaining constable. 'You, check the cellar. And get your truncheon out, just in case.'

Producing an ugly device commonly known as a *life preserver*, the man searched for and found a small doorway set into — and rather effectively hidden — the wall under the stairway. Opening it, he peered down. 'Dark down here, sir,' he called back.

'Then use a bloody torch!' the inspector demanded.

'We have electricity,' Bella said, meekly. 'There is a cord by the door.'

The constable found and pulled it, causing an illumination to appear in the dark cellar, into which he descended.

Nobody spoke a word for the next several minutes while the policemen conducted their searches. Then the one who had been dispatched to the back returned, with a startled-looking Missy in tow. 'Found her in the kitchen, sir,' he said, before exiting to resume his search.

'Indeed?' the inspector growled. 'And who might you be, my girl?'

'This is my maid,' I answered for her. 'She is travelling with me, and helping Bella out in the house.'

Never taking his eyes off the frightened maid, Inspector McCallum said, 'Is that right?'

'Yes sir,' Missy managed to answer. 'Would anyone like any tea?'

'What I'd like is to find a murderer,' the inspector growled. 'Since I doubt you can help me with that, miss, you can go back to your chores.' Missy was only too glad to return to the kitchen.

Meanwhile, Bella, Mr. Creach and I waited in tense silence until the same constable, a tough-looking fellow with a serious face, returned from the back yard. 'No one there, sir.'

'Right,' the inspector muttered.

The second of the policemen came down the stairs to report the same thing: no sign of the prisoner — or anyone, for that matter — hiding under the furniture or in any of the wardrobes.

The third constable emerged from the cellar looking rather startled. He held something in his hands. 'I think you'd better see this, sir,' he said breathlessly.

Walking towards the inspector slowly, as though he was afraid to drop whatever he was holding, but at the same time holding it out as though he could barely bring himself to touch it, the young constable presented his offering almost as a gift — which is exactly how the inspector received it.

'Hel-*lo*,' the inspector intoned, that grin reappearing on his face. 'This is very interesting indeed.' He took the object from the constable and held it up for all of us to see.

Even though my husband is a physician, I have never particularly cared to accompany him to the consulting rooms of his surgery or to any of the hospitals he frequents. I am afraid I lack the stomach for watching body parts being distressed, even though I know it is a necessary step for returning the patient to health. It was therefore with considerable uneasiness that I viewed the thing that had been brought up from the Standishes' cellar, the thing that Inspector McCallum was now virtually thrusting into our faces like some kind of deranged trophy — a human skull.

'Oh, I see you've found Rupert,' Bella commented.

'Rupert?' Mr. Creach and I said in unison.

'What we seem to have found is the remains of a dead man,' Inspector McCallum said, 'and by the looks of it, one that was sent to his grave with a little help.' He turned the skull in such a way as to reveal the back of the cranium. On its top, right about where the crown in the hair would have been, was a rough jagged hole, made as though from a blow. 'Blunt object, I'd say,' the inspector went on. 'Now then, what do you know about this Rupert bloke? Take notes, Sergeant.'

'I don't know very much about him, Inspector,' Bella said, rising, 'except that my husband found him somewhere on a dig and decided to keep it. He has had him for years, long before we were married. He is the one who gave him the name Rupert.'

The inspector levelled a menacing gaze at Bella, who shrank back. 'All right, I'll make a deal with you: you tell me where your husband is hiding right now, and I won't haul you in for harbouring the bones of a dead man in your cellar.'

'What?' Bella exclaimed, looking alarmed.

'Oh, good Lord, McCallum,' Geoffrey Creach said, 'anyone with half a brain can see that is a relic some hundreds, if not thousands, of years old, and not a recent victim of mayhem.'

Though clearly out-argued, the inspector

was not going down gracefully. 'Oh, so it's a relic, eh?' he sneered. 'And how do we know that?'

'I told you,' Bella began, 'Ronnie ... '

'Oh, right, Ronnie. You expect me to take the second-hand testimony of a murderer.'

'Of a suspect,' Mr. Creach corrected. 'And no, I do not expect you to take his word for it. It will be a very simple matter to take that skull to a professor of archaeology in any university in the land and have it examined to find out how old it really is. I could do it for you.'

'The hell you will! I'll hold onto this. This is evidence.'

'Perhaps you should check the body of George Frankham to satisfy yourself that it is not his!' Mr. Creach said, his voice dripping sarcasm.

A satisfied, ugly smile broke out on the inspector's face. 'Yes, I just might do that.'

'Oh, good heavens!' I cried. 'Inspector, your men have searched the premises and have found no one. Aren't there other duties that you and your men must attend to?'

The boulder-shaped creature glared at me. 'Do I make you nervous?' he asked, smiling cruelly.

Irritated beyond reason was probably a better description, but I kept the thought to myself, instead saying: 'I fear your continued presence is upsetting to Mrs. Standish.' Bella looked up at me like a lost fawn.

'Oh, well, now, I wouldn't want that,' Inspector McCallum said, with a total lack of sincerity. 'I'll be off, but I'm going to keep a man posted outside the house here, day and night; and if he sees anyone that might be Standish coming to this house, I'll have my entire force down here before any of you have time to blink.'

Within seconds, blessedly, he and his men were gone. Pulling back the closed curtains and peering outside, I could see him surrounded by the reporters, showing off 'Rupert' to the reporters' obvious delight.

'Dear God,' I muttered. 'How in heaven's name did that man become a police inspector? Does the city hold a lottery?'

'Bath is not exactly a hotbed of crime, Mrs. Watson,' Mr. Creach answered. 'For your standard theft, trespassing or burglary cases, McCallum's oxen-in-a-bottle-factory approach sometimes works. His tendency to bully confessions out of petty criminals has got him where he is. But now, with this murder case, he is grievously in over his head, and what's more, he knows it. Then the circumstantial case against Standish is delivered to him and he realises this is his chance to look competent. But then the pigeon, as it were, flees the coop, and he looks like a fool again. He has to retake Standish and make certain that he is never able to escape again.'

'How? By keeping him in chains?'

'What I fear, Mrs. Watson, is that something might happen to ensure that Standish not only never escapes, but never sees trial and the possibility of acquittal. An accident, shall we say?'

'Oh, really, you cannot be serious. You believe the police would go so far as to try and do away with him?'

'If he were to die before trial, he would die a guilty man in the eyes of everyone.'

Bella put her hands to her head and screamed: 'Stop it! Please, stop! Can't we talk about something else? Anything else?'

Mr. Creach ran to her. 'I wish we could, Bella, but I have to consider every possibility. That is the only way to help Ronnie. I am sorry I spoke so callously just now. You should go back up to bed and rest.'

'No,' she said, unsteadily, 'I don't want to.'

'Mr. Creach,' I said, putting an arm around the girl, 'is there any legal reason that Bella must stay in the house?'

He shook his head. 'Except for the problems she just mentioned, she is free to go. Why? Are you suggesting we slip her over the back fence too?'

'No, I am not.' I had another idea. I called for Missy, who reluctantly came into the room.

'Has that loud man left, mum?' she asked.

'Yes, come here, please, dear.' Missy came over and I took the dishtowel from her and instructed her to stand straight and still. She did, though with obvious confusion. Then I went to Bella and gently pulled her up out of the chair. I walked Bella over to Missy and stood her beside the girl.

'Stand up straight,' I ordered, and when both of the young women did, I was satisfied that the plan forming in my mind was worth chancing. 'Bella, would you like to come and stay with me at my hotel house for a day or so?'

'The reporters would only follow us there, wouldn't they?' she asked.

'Not if they did not realise that it was you.'

I looked at the two girls side by side. Missy was a bit taller, and her hair slightly darker. Bella's build was more slender, and her complexion paler. Despite that, however, there was enough similarity between them to convince me that my plan would work, at least for a while. And perhaps a while was long enough.

'Bella, I would like you to open your wardrobe to Missy,' I said. 'And Missy, please remove your clothes and give them to Bella.'

'My clothes, mum?'

'Yes, dear, I am going to take Bella, in disguise, back to Mrs. Grimes' boarding house with me.'

'Ahh,' Mr. Creach uttered. 'Clever

indeed. I doff my hat to you, Mrs. Watson.'

Bella seemed less than convinced. 'You want me to pose as your maid?' she asked. 'Will this work?'

'If we run quickly enough past them,' I replied. 'The reporters will most likely be looking at me, not my travelling companion. If Mr. Creach escorts us out, he will likewise deflect the attention of the pressmen.'

'I would not miss this little deception for the world,' he said.

'Then the two of you, go and exchange clothing,' I commanded, 'and hurry.'

Once they had gone up the stairs, I said, 'We will need another cab for this, so Bella can dash inside and hide.'

'I will go and hail one then,' Mr. Creach declared, making me begin to wonder how the public transit system in Bath would survive without this man. From outside I heard a cry of 'Look, there's the lawyer!' and the sudden din of a dozen more shouted questions. I was glad that he was braving the mob and not I.

Within a couple of minutes Bella and Missy had re-emerged, and I honestly have to admit that the substitution of Bella for my maid would not for a moment have fooled anyone who knew Missy. We were, however, not trying to fool anyone who knew her, but rather a group of men who had only seen her fleetingly, and very likely remembered nothing more than her clothing.

Geoffrey Creach came back inside and announced that the cab was waiting outside. 'I hope this works,' he said, adding: 'The lions are starting to circle.'

I turned to Missy, who was packed rather tightly into Bella's clothing. 'My dear, I am afraid I am going to have to leave you here for at least a day. I am confident you will be able to find things to do.'

'By myself, mum?' she asked apprehensively.

'I cannot see any other alternative,' I said. 'I will return sometime tomorrow, and by then I may have a new plan.'

'Yes'm,' she muttered, unenthusiastically.

'Perhaps I could ask my fiancée if she would be interested in staying here with the girl,' Mr. Creach said.

'Your fiancée? Congratulations, Mr. Creach. Do you think she would be willing?'

'Oh, I do daresay. She is constantly complaining that I am never available to do anything, so this will give her something to do while I am gone. Besides,' he added in a lower voice, 'she will be able to serve as my eyes and ears while the police are encamped out there. Any sign of trouble and she will know how to contact me.'

'I see,' I said, John and I having worked together in similar fashion on occasion. 'Very well. Let us go then.'

'Wait a minute,' Bella said. 'What if Ronnie comes here and I am gone?'

'I would think that is highly unlikely,' Mr. Creach said. 'But just in case he does, and gets past the reporters, Mrs. Watson's maid will be able to fill him in as to your whereabouts.'

'But if he doesn't come here, where will he go?' Bella protested.

'That is tomorrow's problem,' I said. 'We can only handle one crisis at a time.' Handing over my handkerchief, I instructed Bella to keep it to her face, and perhaps fabricate a sneeze every few seconds. Then, with Mr. Creach taking the lead, we marched out of the house and into the circus.

The reporters did indeed swarm all around us, though as I had predicted, they were more interested in Mr. Creach and myself than in my maid. Bella, in fact, made it all the way to the hansom, which had pulled up at the kerb across the street, without even having to sneeze.

'C'mon, lady, who are you?' one of the reporters demanded as I made my way through the crowd more leisurely. 'What's your business at the murder house?'

I stopped and faced them, allowing Bella to creep into the cab. 'The murder house?' I said. 'I was not aware that a murder had taken place here.'

'That skull the coppers found looked pretty dead to me,' another one said.

'That was a relic,' Mr. Creach replied. 'Likely from a more civilised era, before there were reporters.'

'Give us a break, ducks, tell us who you are!' another reporter shouted.

'Someone who believes that a man is innocent until proven guilty by a jury of his peers,' I called back. 'Even if police and the press do not.'

'Why don't you believe in identifying yourself, then?'

'Don't do it, madam,' Mr. Creach said in a low voice, but it was time to stop being coy.

'Very well. My name is Mrs. Amelia Watson, and I reside in London. I am an old friend of Mrs. Standish, and I have come here to see her. Now, if you please, get out of my way, and if the blood that flows through your veins has not become too polluted with printer's ink, you will begin to leave Mrs. Standish alone as well. She is guilty of nothing except loving her husband, no matter what his predicament.'

I made my way towards the cab, followed by some of the reporters, but was gratified that the shouted questions ceased. I had no trouble entering the cab, where Bella was crouched away from the window, still with the handkerchief to her face.

Mr. Creach leaned in to quickly ask where we were staying, and then turned back to face the mob, as the cab pulled away from the kerb.

'I cannot thank you enough, Miss Pet…Amelia,' Bella said. The effect of being out of her house appeared to have lightened her spirits considerably, and the girl spent the rest of the journey babbling about everything under the sun, things that she had not been allowed to voice since the beginning of her ordeal, and in the process becoming quite schoolgirlish again. I was able to take in only half of what she was saying, my mind instead occupied by my first remarkable day in the city of Bath. I hoped that subsequent days would be rather less eventful.

Arriving back at the hotel, I paid the driver and took Bella inside.

Mrs. Grimes was puzzled at first, even a bit glum, though I suppose that could be attributed to disappointment over losing her newfound help around the house. But once Bella began talking to the landlady, that odd, girlish charm of hers won her over. Since there was more than one empty room in the hotel, Mrs. Grimes graciously agreed to let Bella have a room of her own, rather than forcing her into the servant's cot in my room.

After enjoying a light supper, not terribly well-prepared by Mrs. Grimes, I went to bed early that evening. Bella had requested a meal in her room, where she remained. I was exhausted, but felt a sense of satisfaction that I had managed to take action that had somewhat eased the desperate situation.

And then, sometime in the middle of the night, I awoke, lurching upright in bed.

The night was as quiet as it was dark. It was not anything from the outside that had awakened me, only a bit of knowledge — a supposition, really ... oh, very well, a *deduction* — that had floated to the top of my consciousness as I slept.

All weariness was driven out of me at once. Quickly dressing in the dark, I crept out of my room, down the stairs, and, as silently as I could, opened the front door of the house.

I nearly jumped back out of my boots upon hearing a voice say: 'Who is there?'

Turning, I saw a figure coming towards me in the darkness. 'Is that you, Mrs. Grimes?' I asked.

'No.'

It was Bella, still in her nightdress.

'Dear me, child, you scared five years out of my life,' I moaned. 'What are you doing up?'

'I could not sleep, so I came down to the parlour. But where are you going at this time of night?' she asked.

'I think it is about time that I had a talk with your husband.'

'Ronnie? You mean —'

'Yes, Bella, I have worked out where he is hiding.'

5

'I must go with you!' the girl shouted.

'Bella, please, be quiet,' I cautioned. 'It is still the middle of the night. Get dressed, quickly and quietly, and we shall go.'

She raced up the stairs quickly, but hardly quietly. I could only hope that, after a hard day's work, Mrs. Grimes slept soundly. Bella returned only a few minutes later, her bodice incorrectly buttoned and her shoes not completely laced, but eager beyond words to see her husband. As silently as possible I opened the front door and we stepped out. Only when the door closed behind us did I realise that we had no way of getting back in, since Mrs. Grimes had not provided a key. Perhaps I was not so starkly awake as I had imagined. Well, that would be a problem for later.

The night was cool, but not uncomfortably cold. 'Is it possible to get a cab at this time of night?' I asked Bella, inwardly wondering how the public transport industry in Bath had survived prior to my arrival.

'I don't know, I've never tried,' she said. 'Where is it we're going?'

'The home of George Frankham.'

'That is where Ronnie is?'

'It is the only thing that makes sense,' I said. 'Ronnie cannot go to his own house because the police are watching. I believe they are watching every house in the city except Mr. Frankham's.'

'Why not his?'

'Because as far as the police are concerned, the investigation there is over. They are convinced they have their man and their evidence, so there is no need to keep vigil. I was there earlier today, and there was no trace of a constable to be seen. But we are wasting time. If a cab is impossible, we must walk.'

Indeed, I saw no signs of life on the dark street other than ourselves, so we began walking. Before long we had reached the centre of town, and seeing Bath Abbey emblazoned with light from within, I at once understood the building's appellation 'The Lantern of the West'. It was as awesome a sight as any I have seen.

As I stood admiring it, I heard the sound of a cab coming up behind us. I stopped and bade Bella to halt, all the while praying the driver would not be my 'friend', the oaf from whom I could not seem to get away. To my eternal gratitude, it was not.

'Are you engaged?' I called out.

'Off-duty, ma'am,' the man replied. 'Out a bit late, aren't you, ladies?'

'This is something of an emergency,' I said. 'If you could take us to Ashdown Crescent, we would be most grateful. You see we were, um, visiting a friend, and our hansom did not turn up.'

The cabman, an older fellow with white hair poking out from under his battered tall hat, sighed heavily. 'Get in, it's on my way.' Thanking him, I dashed inside and bade Bella follow me, and soon we were listening to the rhythmic hoofbeats that carried us to our destination. Bella, however, sat huddled on the seat next to me, as though frightened.

'I hope this was the right thing to do,' she said.

'You want to see Ronnie, don't you?'

'Of course, but what must that driver be thinking?'

'He's thinking he has an unexpected fare.'

'No, I mean, what if he thinks we are ...'

'We are what?'

'You know ... professional women. Didn't you see his expression when he asked why we were out so late?'

I could not stifle the laugh. 'What if he does?' I replied.

'He might report us.'

'Oh, good heavens, Bella, report us to *whom*?'

'I don't know. That awful policeman, maybe.'

'I am not worried, dear.'

'All right. But are you certain Ronnie will be there?'

'Trust me, dear, he is there.' Inwardly, I prayed I was right.

The streets of Bath past midnight being largely unpopulated meant that our journey did not take long, and within minutes we were in Ashdown Crescent.

The home of George Frankham was completely dark, but so were most of the others on the street. There was nothing really to distinguish it from its neighbours.

Once the cab had clopped its way out of sight, I said, 'This way,' and led Bella to the door in the wall. Opening it slowly, we both saw a small, dim, flickering light — a candle, no doubt — and in the murky illumination it gave off we could make out a cramped shadow close to the ground.

'Is it —' Bella said, and in an instant, the light was snuffed out.

'It is all right, Mr. Standish,' I called into the darkness. 'Bella is here.'

'Ronnie, is that you?' she cried.

'Keep your voices down!' came the reply in a hushed, but imperative, voice. Then a match was struck and the candle relit, and the flickering fairy light came forth once more. The light came closer, and before long, I could make out the image of a young man.

'Ronnie!' Bella cried, ignoring his pleas for quiet, as the two ran into each other's arms.

'Oh, Bella,' he responded, careful to hold the candle away from her back. 'How I've missed you! But what are you doing here?' Then he glanced up at me. 'And who is this?'

'I am Mrs. Amelia Watson, and I am a friend,' I told him.

'You have heard me speak of her, Ronnie,' Bella said. 'Amelia was my governess ages ago.'

'Not *that* many years ago, child,' I bristled. Honestly, the girl was making it sound as though I had helped Dr. Johnson compile the first dictionary. 'Mr. Standish, shouldn't we perhaps get out of the public eye and ear?'

'I doubt anyone is up at this hour,' he said, 'that is why I choose this time to work, but it probably would be wise to step inside. Follow me, and mind the trenches.'

He led us through his excavation site and into the Frankham house. In the dim light of the lamp I could see that the place was lavishly furnished and decorated in dark colours: earthy greens, browns and rusts. A large painting of a man hung over the fireplace, and the mantel was lined with gold and silver-framed sketches and photographs, as were most of the tables and bookshelf tops as well. Glancing from one picture to the next and comparing it with the painting, I saw that they were all images of the same man at different ages, starting at childhood, moving through school years and then middle age. The man's body thickened and his clothing changed from picture to picture, but one thing remained constant: the haughty look of superiority that revealed itself at every age. The man must have been born with it, like a caul of condescension.

'Mr. Frankham, I presume,' I muttered.

'That is he,' Ronnie said, tensely.

'Ronnie, where did you get those clothes?' Bella asked him, and for the first time I noticed that he was wearing a fine linen shirt, on the breast of which was an odd monogram design that resembled a fish, and a well-tailored pair of trousers, rather too big for him.

'These are Frankham's,' he replied. 'I took them out of his bedroom. He won't be needing them anymore, and the clothes I had been wearing since my arrest were positively vile.'

'Should you really be here, Ronnie?' Bella asked. 'What if you were caught?'

'What could the police do to me that is worse than what I have already endured?'

Ronald Standish was indeed a strapping

young man, with powerful arms on a lean frame, and an intelligent expression on his face. As he lit a small gas lantern, turning the wick down to the lowest setting, I realised that I had better learn as much about him as I could before I had my judgment of him clouded by friendship. I decided upon what I believe is called, in the vernacular of American penny dreadful fiction, an ambush. 'Tell me, Ronnie,' I began sweetly, 'why did you murder Mr. Frankham?'

He spun around and glared at me, an expression of shock, dusted with anger, on his face. 'You too?' he cried. 'I did not kill George Frankham! I know nothing of his death! Must I now declare this to strangers in the street as well as the police?'

'You must to me, if I am to be of any help to you.'

His eyes bored into me. 'I did not kill George Frankham!' he shouted. 'I did not see him that night, I was not with him that night, I did not speak to him that night. How can I make myself any clearer?'

'Ronnie, please, control yourself,' Bella implored, rushing to him. To me, she said: 'Under normal circumstances, Amelia, he is the mildest of men.'

I smiled and walked towards him. 'Which is exactly what has convinced me of his innocence,' I said. 'It is my belief that the only people who would *not* become angry by such a direct accusation are guilty, for they are more interested in coming up with a convincing story. Conversely, when you accuse an innocent person of a crime, shock, anger or outrage is generally the response. It was exactly what I was looking for.'

Ronnie relaxed and mopped his brow with his sleeve. 'Thank you ... I think.'

As I returned my gaze to the fireplace, I noticed something interesting. 'Look at this,' I said, 'one picture is missing.'

'What?'

I pointed to a gap in the line of frames on the mantel, which resembled nothing so much as a lost tooth in a silver and gold smile.

'Perhaps he moved it somewhere else.' Ronnie shrugged. 'Or perhaps he was anticipating a new one and left an opening for it.'

'Perhaps,' I said, making a cursory

examination of the fireplace. At the very bottom of the hearth I thought I caught a tiny glistening. 'May I have the lamp, please?' I asked, taking it from Ronnie and carrying it over to the fireplace. 'Mmm-hmm,' I uttered.

'What is it?' Bella asked.

Careful not to spot my dress with ash or soot, I reached into the hearth and pulled out a gilded picture frame. 'It looks as though someone tried to bury it in the fire logs and ash.' Taking the frame over to the light, I saw that the picture had been torn out; all that remained of it was a small triangle lodged in one corner, protected by a shard of glass. Carefully removing it, I examined it thoroughly, noticing that there was a scrawl of ink on the back. 'Something is written on this.'

'Let me see,' Ronnie said, coming over to examine it. 'It looks like the letters *i*, *c* and *e* — 'ice' — on one line; and underneath it *h*, *e* and *r* — 'her' — and below that, *l*, *e*, then *s* and *t*. 'Lest'?'

I looked at the scrap of paper once more, and concurred with his reading. The visible letters read:

ice
her
le st.

It made no sense, of course, though the full stop after the *t* indicated that it was the end of a sentence, which indicated that in its unabridged form, it was a complete thought. The space between the '*le*' and '*st*' was rendered quite puzzling by this interpretation, unless it was not a deliberate space but the product of carelessness.

Bella rushed up to look at the sliver of paper. 'Is this what policemen call a clue?' she asked, excitedly.

'Yes, dear, this is a clue, though what it might lead to I cannot imagine.'

'Whatever was in that photograph, Frankham clearly wanted to obliterate it,' Ronnie reasoned.

'No, not Mr. Frankham,' I said. 'Had there been something he considered dangerous or incriminating to him, he never would have put it up in the first place. Someone else removed this photograph, quite quickly, and then attempted to hide the frame.'

'Who?' Bella asked.

'The murderer, perhaps? What if there were something in the photograph that would point to the identity of Frankham's killer, and that is why he had to remove it?'

'But why not just take it with him? Why try to hide it?'

'Why indeed, and in such a clumsy fashion? That argues that it must have been someone who was not supposed to be in this house and had limited time, out of fear of getting caught.' I glanced over at Ronnie.

'Don't look at me that way,' he said. 'I have no idea what was in that photograph. Besides, if I had wanted to get rid of it for whatever reason, I would have had plenty of time to do a more thorough job of it. I have been here for hours.'

'True enough,' I acknowledged, glancing once more at the tiny puzzle piece before slipping it into my handbag. 'And now I suppose we must work out what to do with you.'

'You are not going to turn him back over to the police!' Bella cried.

'No, I am not. If Inspector McCallum cannot follow the same deduction that I did and find Ronnie on his own, I am not going to help him.'

'Then I suppose he could simply stay here?'

'I suppose, but —'

'There are stores in the kitchen,' Ronnie interrupted. 'I could actually stay here for several days.'

'Well —'

'And I could stay with him!' Bella crowed.

'No, dear, that would be taking an enormous risk,' I cautioned.

'It is one I will take, gladly, as long as I can be with Ronnie.' Now that they had been reunited I could see that there would be no real way to separate them again. Perhaps my bringing them together was a tactical error. Even if it was, there was clearly nothing I could do now to rectify it.

'Very well, though I hope you know what you are doing,' I told her.

A nearby church bell chimed three o'clock. 'Oh, good heavens, half the night is gone. I will leave you two to each other and pray that it will be enough to keep you safe. I will not volunteer any information as to your whereabouts to the inspector, though if I am directly questioned about it, and there is no way out, I will not be able to lie about it. I am sure you understand that, Bella.'

'Yes, of course,' she muttered glumly.

'Good. I will try to make it back here tomorrow to check on the two of you. And please, be discreet. Don't let yourselves be seen during the day.'

'We won't, Amelia,' Bella promised. 'And thank you.'

'Yes, thank you,' Ronnie echoed.

'I will find my own way out,' I said, and took my leave.

Outside, the night seemed cooler than it had been on the journey up here, and there was no cab in sight. Still, it was not an unpleasant night, so I walked back to the Roman Hotel, seeing no one except for an odd figure or two on the streets, arriving just before the clock struck half-past three. There was no light or sound downstairs, and I had no way of getting in. There was nothing for it but to ring the bell.

On the third try, I heard Mrs. Grimes' voice on the other side of the door call out: 'I'm coming, I'm coming!' The door was quickly unlocked and wrenched open and the fatigued-looking woman cried, ''Tis closed we are, what'll you be wantin' ... Mrs. Watson? What are you doing out?'

'Mrs. Grimes, please forgive me,' I began, stepping inside, 'but I just couldn't sleep.'

'Oh. Well, I suppose I can turn the mattress tomorrow —'

'No, no, it has nothing to do with the bed, the bed is lovely. It's just, well, being in a new place and all that. I thought perhaps if I went out for a walk it would relax me enough to sleep. But I simply lost track of the time. I am sorry.'

She yawned. 'Well, no harm done, though I won't be expecting you early in the morning for breakfast.'

'Thank you for understanding,' I said, making my way upstairs. Once in my room I quickly undressed and climbed into bed.

I slept comfortably and dreamlessly, and did not awaken the next morning until forced to do so by an insistent pounding on my door.

'Mrs. Watson,' Mrs. Grimes called, 'are

you awake?'

'What?' I muttered, trying to collect my thoughts.

'Mrs. Watson?'

'Yes, I am awake,' I said, getting up and quickly throwing on my dressing gown, then opening the door to the landlady, who appeared distressed. 'Is something wrong?'

A cry came from downstairs: 'Is she up there or not?'

Mrs. Grimes turned and hollered back: 'Ah, pipe down, the lot o' you!' Then she came into the room and slammed the door shut.

'What in heaven's name is going on?' I asked.

'The press hounds,' she spat. 'Showed up this morning, they did, all looking for you. I didn't mind it much at first, figuring if there's writin' to be done, they could go ahead and write about the hotel. Maybe it'll improve business. But I won't stand by while they try breakin' into my guests' rooms!'

'Why do they want me?'

'I'm sure I don't know, though I'm guessin' it has something to do with you bein' in tight with Sherlock Holmes.'

'Oh, good heavens! How did they find that out? Did you tell them?'

'Not I.'

I sat back down on the bed and sighed. There was nothing I could do with the press except face them. I could hardly be expected to spend the entire day in this room. Besides, there was another errand I wanted to run in the city, a visit to the local library. 'Please give me a few minutes for my toilet and to get dressed, and I shall be down to talk to them.'

'All right, ma'am.' She turned to leave.

'One more thing, Mrs. Grimes? There is no need to mention to them that Mrs. Standish is here, or to involve her in any of this.'

''Tis not her they've been askin' about.'

'Good. I doubt you will see her today, either. Please don't disturb her room.'

The landlady blindly agreed, for which I was grateful, since I did not want to explain *why* she would not be seeing Bella today.

Washing and dressing quickly, I went downstairs and discovered only four men, each of whom looked familiar from the crowd that had been outside the Standishes' yesterday, all waiting and pacing in the parlour of the boarding house. Upon spotting me, they jumped up and began shouting out questions. I raised my hand to silence them.

'Gentlemen, I have not yet had my breakfast,' I said. 'If you are willing to wait until I am finished, or are willing to join me, I will give you a statement.'

That appeared to catch them by surprise, and they looked from one to another until one, a young fellow in a red plaid, tweed cap said, 'I'll have a cup of coffee, if you please.'

Another one, who was much older and wore a bemused expression, chimed in: 'I wouldn't say no to an egg and a sausage.' The remaining two readily agreed.

'I feel certain that Mrs. Grimes would be willing to accommodate you all with breakfast — for a fair price each, of course.' I stole a look at the landlady, whose careworn face suddenly broke into a grin.

'Come on, lads,' the first journalist called to the others, moving into the dining room. 'We can't refuse such a kind invitation as this.'

Once seated, I learned that the elder reporter, a Mr. Bryce, worked for the *Police Gazette*, while the plaid-capped youngster, a certain Peter Poole, was a representative of the local newspaper. The other two were somewhat less communicative about themselves. Before long, Mrs. Grimes brought in the breakfast plates and, after happily collecting a sixpence from each, said, 'I'll leave you to it, then,' and left the room.

'Very well then,' I began. 'First, some basic facts: as you most likely know already, I am the wife of Dr. John H. Watson of London.'

'We've already confirmed that,' Mr. Bryce said, 'but why are you here?'

'I am here because of a letter written by Mrs. Bella Standish, who was a pupil of mine some twenty years ago. I am offering Bella moral support through her ordeal.'

'Is Sherlock Holmes going to take on the case?' asked Peter Poole.

'No. I have not been in contact with Mr. Holmes. I have not seen him or spoken to him for quite some time.'

'What about Dr. Watson?'

'John is otherwise engaged at present.'

'Mrs. Watson, have you seen and spoken with Ronald Standish since you have been here?' Mr. Bryce asked.

From the entryway a new voice said: 'How could she have? Mr. Standish escaped from gaol shortly after her arrival, and remains at large.'

The reporters turned to see the speaker: Geoffrey Creach.

'Mr. Creach, I did not hear you come in,' I said.

The solicitor looked at me with an expression of mild annoyance and announced: 'Gentlemen, I am sorry to inform you that this press conference is over. Mrs. Watson has an appointment at police headquarters.'

'I do?'

'Indeed, madam. The order came from Inspector McCallum himself, who contacted me and ordered — not asked, not requested, not instructed, but *ordered* — me to bring you there myself. He was quite agitated.'

'More so than usual?'

'Much more so. For a moment I thought that he was going to literally explode.'

119

'Oh, very well.' Rising and turning to the reporters, I said, 'Good day, gentlemen. Do enjoy the remainder of your breakfast.'

Over their protests, Mr. Creach hustled me out to a waiting cab and we set off for the police station. 'Do you have any idea what this is about?' I asked.

'Not really, except that you have done something to make the inspector very angry.'

'Oh,' I muttered, immediately assuming the worst: that the authorities had found the Standishes at the Frankham house and had extracted from Bella the story of how I had shuttled her around from place to place like a chess piece. Then again, if the police had recaptured Ronnie, wouldn't Geoffrey Creach know of it?

At the police station we got out of the cab and walked inside, past a few milling uniformed officers, and into the office of Inspector McCallum. The inspector was seated at his desk, upon which stacks of papers were neatly arranged, one of which was being held down by a half-empty bottle of stout.

'Good morning, Inspector,' I said, mustering up a pleasantness that I did not feel.

'What did you want to see me about?'

Inspector McCallum looked up and I could see at once that my attempt at conviviality was a wasted effort.

'You've not been honest with me, woman,' he declared. 'You've played me for a fool.'

'Inspector McCallum, I have no idea what you are talking about.'

'Oh no? You failed to point out the little fact that you was related to *the* Dr. Watson of bleeding Baker Street when we first met.'

'I am not actually related to him, I am married to him. And now that you have found out, I fail to see what it has to do with anything.'

'What it has to do?' he screamed, reddening. 'A line of reporters was in here this morning, all barking out questions about whether Sherlock bloody Holmes is going to be called in! And me standing there like a bloody fool, without the faintest notion of what they're talking about. It was the newshounds what told me about you and Sherlock Holmes!'

How had the reporters found that out so quickly? Could it have been Missy? No, she has not been in contact with any one … unless she had spoken to PC Richter at the Standishes' house. But if she had done that, the inspector would surely know by now that Bella was no longer in the house. As I pondered this, my words of the day before to the pack of newsmen suddenly came back to me: *My name is Mrs. Amelia Watson and I reside in London. I* was the one who had told them! I had given them all the information they needed to send a telegram or place a telephone call to any one of the newspapers in London for confirmation of John's — and my — identity. Oh, dear.

'Are you listening to me?' the inspector was now screaming, which shook me out of my ponderings.

'What?' I asked. 'Inspector, if you would speak a bit more softly, I believe I would hear much more.'

His feral eyes moved back and forth between Mr. Creach and me. 'Fine, here's the point,' he said, softly, but with dangerous intensity. 'I am in charge of this investigation, and I am not about to have anyone getting in my way. Not you, not

Sherlock bloody Holmes, not Scotland bleeding Yard, nobody!' Then he levelled a finger at Mr. Creach. 'And not you, either. Have I made myself clear?'

'You have made yourself far more than clear,' I replied, as calmly as I could. 'I have no desire whatsoever to get in your way. My primary concern is for Bella Standish, and my primary hope is that her husband is treated fairly and openly by the rule of law.'

The inspector glared at me until Mr. Creach burst in: 'Will there be anything else, Inspector?'

'No,' he growled, reaching for the stout bottle. 'Get out of my sight.'

That was Inspector McCallum's polite and charming way of releasing us. I walked out with Mr. Creach into the bright daylight, not only disgusted and angry, but also plagued with a sensation of guilt; for, despite the inspector's subhuman demeanour, I could not deny that he had been correct in his charge that I was not being completely honest. Certainly not regarding the whereabouts of Ronnie Standish. The least I could do now, it seemed, was be honest with the solicitor.

'Mr. Creach,' I said, 'would it help or hinder the situation if you knew where Ronnie Standish was?'

'It would help, of course,' he said, eyeing me. Then his eyes narrowed. 'Mrs. Watson, what are you keeping from me?'

Taking a deep breath, I told him. Geoffrey Creach's reaction was at first surprise, but a knowing roll of the eyes quickly followed that. 'Of course, that makes perfect sense,' he said. 'I am ashamed for not having deduced that myself. Was it you who recommended that he go there?'

'No, not at all. I discovered him there last night.'

'What were you doing at Frankham's house last night?'

'I was acting upon a hunch.'

'And does Bella know?'

'Yes, she was with me. In fact, I left her there.'

A look of concern crossed his face. 'Was that wise?'

'Mr. Creach, I could not have separated them with ropes and elephants.'

The solicitor sighed. 'I suppose not. Still,

Bella should not stay there any longer than necessary. I will stop by later today and talk to them. Until then, Mrs. Watson, I would advise you to take caution. Your impromptu news conference this morning will likely make headlines, which will do nothing to assure McCallum that you are endeavouring to stay out of his way. From now on, I would try to avoid talking with the press.'

'I shall do my best,' I told him, 'though they are not exactly easy to avoid. But I wonder if you might do something for me, Mr. Creach.'

'What?'

'Direct me to the library.'

'Library?'

'Yes. I am fond of libraries.'

'I see. And there is no chance that you are acting upon another of your hunches?'

'In a library?'

'All right.' The solicitor gave me directions to a lending library just across the Pultney Bridge, after which I bade him farewell. I sensed that he did not believe me entirely, which was actually wise on his part, since I was acting upon another hunch, which was that the gold medallion Ronnie had found was at the very heart of Frankham's murder. I was hoping to find a book that contained some reference to it, in order to determine exactly what it was the young man had found.

Following the directions, I arrived some twenty minutes later at the lending library, which was next to a photographer's shop in Argyle Street. I stepped inside to find two small, dark rooms crammed with books, seemingly presided over by a lazy black-and-white cat, which was curled on a small desk. *Meooowwww*, it greeted me.

'Have we a patron, Minerva?' a man's voice called from the back.

Moments later the man emerged. He was the sort of person who might have been fifty but looked eighty, or actually eighty but having retained a spark of youth. If the former, he was certainly in training to be elderly. With his black Victorian-style clothing, his dust-coloured hair, and lean, pale face, which looked like it had not seen the sun in years, he appeared to be a daguerreotype brought to life.

'I don't recall seeing you before,' the man

said in a soft voice.

'I am a visitor to the city,' I replied.

'Oh, oh dear. I shan't be able to lend you a book, then. Minerva and I cater to city residents only, you see.'

'If I find one I like, might I read it here?'

'We are not a reading library, Miss ...'

'Mrs. Amelia Watson.'

'My name is Dawes, Mrs. Watson. Timothy Dawes to Minerva, just plain Dawes to everyone else.'

'I see,' I muttered, wondering what I would say if the strange old fellow would begin referring to the cat as *Mrs. Dawes*.

'I do not wish to be rude, of course,' the man went on, 'so if you tell me what sort of book you are seeking, perhaps we could come to some agreement. We have just got something in called *Chastity Chased Through Cheshire*, which I've not read myself, but which has proven popular.'

Oh, Lord!

'Actually, Mr. Dawes, I have become quite fascinated by the Roman ruins here in town. I was rather hoping you would have a volume that would detail the ancient Roman society.'

127

'Ah, yes. It so happens we do have such a book, but it is not on the shelf.'

'Is it in the back?' I asked.

'No, I'm afraid it has been checked out.'

'When will it return?'

'That is difficult to say,' Mr. Dawes responded. 'It was checked out seven years ago.'

'Seven years? Haven't you tried to get it back?'

'I have sent letters, yes, but the gentleman who took it has not responded. Being a visitor, perhaps you are not familiar with our Lord Beckham.'

'I am afraid not.'

'He is our local peer, a man of great wealth, of great interests and experiences, and, shall we say, unusual tastes. He is reputed to have one of the greatest and most comprehensive private libraries in the world, the kind of collection that could make our humble little collection here considerably less humble.'

I thought I understood how he had assembled his collection.

'It is a collection of which I can only dream,' Mr. Dawes said. 'It is also my hope that someday he may be convinced to will it to the good people of Bath. So you see my predicament.'

I was forced to admit to the man that I did not.

'Pressing his lordship for the return of one book might jeopardise future negotiations for the donation of his entire library.'

While use of the word 'future' seemed more of an expression of optimism for someone I had concluded must have experienced the Georgian era firsthand, I acknowledged his predicament.

'Perhaps I could help,' I said.

'You? How?'

'If the library of this Lord Beckham is as extensive as you say, he no doubt will have the sort of book for which I am looking. I shall therefore visit the man and his collection, and while I am there inquire after your book.'

'Visit? Lord Beckham? At his home?' Mr. Dawes appeared to think this idea was somehow more preposterous than journeying to the moon.

'Surely he is not as unapproachable as that.'

'But he is a peer.'

And I have met the King, I thought, but said nothing.

'I should not want to visit the abbey, he said, shuddering.

'An abbey, you say?'

'A gothic abbey, like something out of Walpole. The perfect place for eldritch and arcane ceremonies held in the dark of night. There are stories of people who have attempted to call on his lordship, only to never be seen again.'

'You know this to be true?' I asked, incredulously.

'One hears things, Mrs. Watson,' Mr. Dawes said, as Minerva, meowed in agreement.

'Now you have piqued my interest. Where might I find the abbey?'

'It is about three miles out of town. No common road goes by the abbey, but if you head north on the Old Road, you will come to a forest grove. There is a service drive that cuts through it. That will lead to the abbey.'

'Thank you for your help and information,' I said, turning and heading for the door. 'Good day, Mr. Dawes.'

'Heed my warning, Mrs. Watson,' he said, grimly. 'Do not go to the abbey.'

As I stepped out of the dark library into the very bright street, a man standing outside of the photographer's shop caught my eye.

'I have time for a sitting this afternoon,' he said. 'Surely there is someone in your life who would appreciate a lovely photograph of you.'

'There is, but not today, I'm afraid,' I replied.

'Another time, then?' the man said, handing me a business card that read *J. Allardice, Photographer.* 'I shall be here when you need me.'

'Thank you,' I said, tucking the card in my handbag and walking past him. On such a cheerfully sunny day, dire warnings of a dark, dank, dangerous abbey inhabited by a mysterious lord seemed so — well, so *fictional* that I had to chuckle at the folly of the old librarian. Heed his warning, indeed! If the answer to my question was at the abode of Lord Beckham, than my pathway seemed clear: I would visit the place at once.

6

If I was going to pay a call at the manor house of Lord Beckham ('gothic abbey' surely being an exaggeration), there was something I needed to take with me: an object that I had to obtain from Bella and Ronnie's house. The walk to Albert Street took no time at all, in part because I was beginning to find my bearings in the city of Bath, but also because my ankle had been exercised back to normal.

Upon arriving at the house, I noticed that the wolf pack was mysteriously absent, though PC Richter remained steadfastly at his post. The absence of the reporters boded well and ill equally: well because it meant that they had gone on to some other story and would no longer be pestering the occupants of the house; ill because I was suddenly fearful that my judgment in leaving Missy there had proven wrong and the press had discovered the substitution. As I walked up to the porch, I noticed that, while still standing upright, PC Richter appeared by be fast asleep and snoring. I gently nudged his arm, and his head popped up immediately. 'What? Hmm? Oh, it's you, ma'am. Good day to you.'

'How are you, Constable?' I said, still marvelling at his ability to doze in an upright position. 'What has happened to the usual chorus of journalists?'

'Must've found the scent o' blood elsewhere,' he sniffed. 'Good riddance, if you ask me.'

'Have you seen Mrs. Standish today?' I inquired, casually, maintaining the fiction that Bella was still within the house.

'No ma'am, very quiet, it's been. Since the arrival o' the other young woman, the solicitor's dolly, I haven't seen anyone.'

'The solicitor's dolly?' I asked, and then I remembered that Geoffrey Creach had offered to have his fiancée come over to keep Missy company.

This created something of a problem, since my reason for returning to the house was to borrow the hidden gold medallion in order to have it perused by Lord Beckham when I paid a call on him. Since Mr. Creach did not know about the medallion's existence, I could hardly pull it out in front of his fiancée and explain my plan. With only Missy in the house, I could always send her on a task and have plenty of time to spirit away the medallion, but how would I be able to get away from the other woman?

'May I go in?' I asked, while I pondered my predicament.

'Of course, ma'am.' PC Richter knocked lightly on the door; a second later, it opened a crack and an unfamiliar voice said, 'Who is it?'

'It's the lady from London,' the constable replied.

'Amelia Watson,' I said.

The door opened enough for me to see a young woman who smiled upon seeing me. 'Oh, yes, Geoffrey told me you might be by. I am Kitty Cornwell. Please come in.'

I have endured, for most of my life, the designation of being 'tall for a woman'. I stand some nine inches over five feet, only an inch or so shorter than my husband. But Kitty Cornwell was nearly as tall as I, and quite thin. Her dark blonde hair was piled high on her head and her dress was of the most nondescript beige. A less charitable person than I might describe her as plain, though her apparent plainness all but disappeared when she smiled, which she was doing now. It was the kind of smile that radiated warmth, and I found myself smiling back as I entered the house.

Missy had certainly been busy during my absence, since the Standish home now looked perfectly kept and neat. As Kitty Cornwell invited me into the day room, where the curtains were still drawn to keep out prying eyes, Missy attended to the teakettle.

'Kitty is a rather unusual name,' I commented.

'My, my given name is Katherine, but I've been called Kitty since I was a girl.'

'How long have you and Mr. Creach been engaged, if you do not mind my asking?'

'Not at all. For a little better than a year now, I'm afraid. To listen to Geoffrey, there is never a right time for the wedding. I thought we were getting close, but now this case has come up and he is all but consumed by it.'

'He indicated that you would serve as his eyes and ears here in regard to the mob outside.'

She sighed. 'There are times when the only way I can see Geoffrey at all is to assist him in his work. What is it about men and their obsessions?'

What indeed?

'Since you are Mr. Creach's designated lookout, do you know why the reporters have left?'

'Have they?' she asked. 'Boredom, perhaps. Or perchance they have to go back and write their stories about nothing.'

'I hope Missy has not been a bother to you.'

'Oh, gracious, no. But is it true that the poor waif's name is really *Mistletoe*?'

'Alas, it is true,' I said.

'And all this time I've disliked *Katherine* because it is so common!'

We both laughed and continued to make pleasant small talk until Missy brought in the tea, along with a small plate of scones. 'Will there be anything else, mum?' she asked.

'Not for the moment, Missy. You have

been extremely busy, why don't you go upstairs and rest for a bit?'

'Oh, I'm not tired, mum.'

Inwardly, I groaned. If I could not even get Missy out of the room, how was I going to get rid of Kitty long enough to spirit away the medallion? Perhaps I should just confess what I was up to and inform Mr. Creach of my suspicions … or perhaps not. The idea came to me at once, and while I had no doubt that it would work, it would also take some skilful acting.

Picking up the teacup, I took a sip and then said, 'You know, what I would really like is a glass of water.'

'Right away, mum,' Missy said, turning around.

'No, no, you stay here, dear, I shall get it myself.'

'But it's no —'

'Missy, when I brought you along on this trip, I envisioned it as a holiday for you as well,' I said. 'The truth is, I feel rather badly about making you work the entire time. You sit here and rest. I assure you I can get a glass of water for myself.'

'All right, mum,' the girl said, taking

a seat, while I hastened to the kitchen. My real reason for wanting to go into the kitchen was not born of thirst, but rather to stage a bit of creative misdirection.

Once there, I shouted: 'You there! Who are you?' loudly enough for it to carry to the day room. 'Get away from here!'

As I had hoped, both Kitty and Missy burst through the kitchen door. 'What is it, Mrs. Watson?' Kitty asked.

'A strange man was outside, peeping through the window!' I cried. It was a complete fabrication, of course, but it was the only way I could keep them out of the day room for the moment I needed. 'He ran towards the fence.'

'Shall I contact Geoffrey?'

'No, but please watch for him while I alert the constable.' With that I ran back out and dashed straight to Ronnie Standish's desk, yanked open the drawer, and pulled out the hidden gold medallion, which I stuffed into my handbag on my way to the door.

'Constable, I saw someone out the back!' I lied.

'Was it one of those reporters?' he asked.

'I don't know. I didn't get a good look.'

'You go inside, I'll check it out.' PC Richter ran around the side of the house to the back yard while I went back inside.

I sat down on the sofa to catch my breath, a respite that lasted only a moment before the next potential opportunity for disaster struck me. 'Missy!' I called, and the girl came running. 'You must go upstairs and hide.'

'Why, mum?'

'Because if Constable Richter sees you, he will wonder who it was who left with me yesterday. He still thinks Bella is here.'

'Ooh, you won't let them take me into the station, will you, mum?'

'It won't come to that if you get upstairs, now go!'

The girl had only just disappeared from sight when a knock came to the door. Kitty now came into the room from the kitchen, a wry smile on her face. 'Shall I answer it?' she asked.

'Please.'

It was, of course, PC Richter, reporting that he had found no trace of anyone out the back. 'But we'll keep an eye on the back too from now on, ma'am,' he said, before returning to his vigil outside.

Heavens, now I had inadvertently closed off Mr. Creach's secret escape route! *Oh, what a tangled web we weave.* 'I hope I haven't created a mess that will come back to haunt all of us,' I moaned.

'Shouldn't your friend Sherlock Holmes be able to clear up any problem?'

'You mean my husband's friend, Kitty.'

She sat down on the sofa next to me. 'Oh? Are there difficulties between you and he?'

'Let me say simply that Mr. Holmes is a trying human being.'

'What does that mean?'

'It means if he tries hard enough, he might actually become one.'

While Kitty chuckled at that, I rose. 'At the risk of seeming rude, I'm afraid I must be going. There is another stop on my itinerary today. Please forgive me. But it was a delight to meet you, Kitty.'

'And you too, Mrs. Watson,' she said.

After calling up to Missy to tell her that I was off again, and to not present herself at windows, I stepped outside and gave another brief thanks to PC Richter, who was now holding his post more diligently — and wide awake — than ever, having been convinced that someone had been skulking around the house.

But as I walked through the city, intent upon my mission, a dark cloud of reality settled upon me: resolving to pay a call upon Lord Beckham was all well and good, but how would I get there? If Mr. Dawes had been right that there was no common road that went to the abbey, then a cab might be out of the question, particularly if the driver was as fearful of the place as the old librarian. Walking was a possibility, though I would really rather not. I did not trust my ankle that much.

Bath, I conceded, was not London, where virtually anywhere was accessible either through a coach, a cab, an omnibus, a boat, or rail transit. It was then that the answer to my problem flew past me on two wheels.

I hastened back to the Roman Hotel to find Mrs. Grimes crouched down and wielding a spade in the front garden. ''Tis enjoyin' the city you've been?' she asked.

'I can honestly say I have never had a

holiday like this one,' I replied. 'Do you by any chance know where I might be able to rent a bicycle?'

'A bicycle, you be wantin',' she said. 'As for rentin' one, I've nary a thought. But I do have one in the shed, should you be wantin' to use it. It belonged to Mr. Grimes, rest his soul.'

'I should very much like to borrow it.'

'Come on, then.'

I followed her out to the back yard, where an old but serviceable bicycle was leaning against a small tool shed. It had been quite some years since the last time I had ridden a bicycle, though I was sure I still knew how, and given the directions that the strange librarian had given me, it would be just the thing for cutting through the green between the roadway and the abbey. 'This will do very well,' I said. 'Do you happen to know how to get to the Old Road?'

'Oh, 'tis easy,' she said, then proceeded to rattle off the directions like an auctioneer. What I drew from her description was that the Old Road basically cut over the top half of the city, so heading north on any major

142

street would eventually deposit me there. Or something like that.

'Thank you, Mrs. Grimes,' I said, climbing aboard the bicycle, taking care to fold the lower half of my dress in such a way that it could not possibly get tangled in the pedal mechanism. My handbag, I held tightly under my arm.

'Will you be back for dinner?' she asked.

'I don't know. I'm eventually going to meet a friend.'

'Hoo! 'Tis a fast worker, ye are. In town a day, and a friend already.'

'It's a mutual friend of mine and Mrs. Standish's,' I lied.

'Right. An' I've heard nary a peep from her room all day.'

'I'm not surprised.'

She moved in close to me. 'I know what you're doin', you know.'

'You do?'

''Tis a case for Sherlock Holmes you're workin'.'

I winked and held a finger up to my lips, and she winked back, as I started to pedal away.

Travelling through Bath by bicycle was

not a particularly easy task, since so many of the streets were still cobbled, but I was pleased to realise that years of inactivity had not deprived me of my skill with a two-wheeled vehicle. I pedalled uphill, past river, gardens and more stone buildings, until I found myself on a wide thoroughfare that had to be Old Road. Upon cresting a hill I was rewarded with a beautiful landscape of green fields dotted with farmhouses separated by rustic stone fences.

From this vantage point it would seem that something as axiomatic as a gothic abbey should be visible, but none could be seen on the horizon. There was, however, a wooded area, as had been described by Mr. Dawes, just off the road ahead.

I pedalled more slowly as I neared the grove, looking for the turn-off drive. Finally I spotted a tamped earth path which led to the woods and turned onto it. The trail — one could hardly call it a drive — was quite rough, which made for a difficult ride, but I could not imagine it being any more pleasant had I been walking.

When I finally got to the woods it appeared that the forest had swallowed me up, bicycle and all. The tall trees all but blocked out the sunlight, suddenly thrusting the woods into an eerie, artificial dusk. An unnatural silence enveloped the place; there was no birdsong, no sounds of insects, only the noises given off by the squeak of the bicycle wheels on the coarse pathway.

Up ahead I could see that the woods broke into a clearing, into which sunlight once more poured, and I was quite relieved to exit the thick wall of trees that obscured it from view on the Old Road. Immediately on the other side was a high stone fence with an ornate, arched gatehouse at its centre. I slowed down, thinking I might confront a guard at the gatehouse; but, sighting none, passed through, pedalling only a few more yards until I had to stop and stand in amazement at what I was seeing.

The librarian's description of the home of Lord Beckham did not begin to do it justice. It was a stone pile unlike anything I had ever encountered. The front was like a cathedral, with an enormous stained glass window placed above the arched door, and on each side were wings the size of housing blocks, one of which had a small, square tower attached to it. Behind the façade was a keep at least four stories tall, not unlike the Tower of London. But its centrepiece was the massive octagonal tower, which rose up out of the structure and lorded over it like the smokestack of a mill, the top of which appeared to be haunted by rooks.

Even more startling than the sheer size of the abbey was its condition: it appeared to be crumbling at every joint, making me wonder how safe it was to live inside, and an unhealthy-looking green moss covered nearly every surface of the first level.

Intoxicated by the sight of the abbey (and totally puzzled as to how an ancient building like this could remain such a secret to the outside world, hidden by a forest or not), I stepped off of the bicycle and pushed it closer to the entry hall — with some measure of trepidation, I have to admit.

Once I got close enough, however, I began to notice oddities about the building. One was that, far from crumbling, the mortar between the stones appeared to be quite new. Another was the moss, which, as I reached out to touch it, I realised was not moss at all but what appeared to be a textured layer of plaster stuck onto the stone and painted green. The building was not an ancient crumbling pile, it was a relatively modern construction!

Leaning the bicycle against the side of the entryway, I approached the vaulted wooden doors, which, like the rest of the surroundings, looked ancient and decaying, though — also like the rest of the surroundings — turned out to be solid oak that was carefully pocked and pitted to give that appearance. There was no visible doorbell, although each door bore a heavy iron knocker that had been cast in the image of a *memento mori*. With some effort I lifted up one of the knockers and let it fall. Moments later the door smoothly swung open and a man stepped out from behind it ... the smallest man I had ever seen, no more than three feet tall.

'May I help you?' he asked.

'I would like to see Lord Beckham,' I told him.

'Why?'

'Well, I ... I would like to show him this.' From my handbag I pulled the gold medallion and handed it to the little man.

'One moment,' he said, disappearing inside with it. He returned less than a minute later. 'Please come in.'

The interior of the building was every bit as spectacular as the exterior, looking more like a cloister than a private residence. The ceilings were tall and vaulted, and the walls of the finest wood panelling. The ornately-carved table near the doorway could have been imported from any one of the royal houses of Europe. There were standing candelabras throughout the entrance hall, but these seemed largely for decoration, since the room was illuminated by electricity. I followed the dwarf through the entrance hall and down a corridor so wide it could have easily accommodated a train, past an enormous, beautifully-woven tapestry appeared to depict the daily life of a culture I could not readily identify, and into a study. I say *study*, though *library* could have just as easily served as a description, as could have *laboratory*.

The walls were not merely lined with shelves, they *were* shelves from floor to ceiling, with the uppermost one reachable only by use of the rolling ladder that was attached to a pipe rail at the very top. In the centre of the room was an enormous globe with tiny paper flags planted, for some reason, on various continents.

From the centre of the ceiling hung a replica of the solar system, and I could not help noticing that, in addition to the eight recognised planets, there were two extra orbs suspended by strings. One corner of the room was obscured by a two-panel screen, though I could see a pipe of some kind rising from behind it and disappearing into the ceiling. In another corner of the room was a harp. The centre of one wall was a gigantic window made up of four vaulted panes, and in front of it was an enormous desk. At least, I believe that it was a desk holding up the mounds of papers and books.

Standing behind the desk (or the heap) was a striking-looking man with steel-grey hair, a whitish beard, and penetrating eyes that were so dark they appeared to be made of coal. Most startlingly, he was wearing a long blue caftan, unbelted, and a military pith helmet. He was holding the medallion.

'Come in, come in,' the man bade in a

commanding voice.

'Lord Beckham?' I inquired.

'If I'm not, I'm certainly enjoying his fortune,' he replied. 'How much?'

'I beg your pardon?'

He held up the medallion. 'How much? You came here to sell it, did you not?'

'I did not.'

'Then why are you here?'

'My lord, I am here on behalf of the wife of Ronald Standish.'

'Are you, now? I have no idea whatsoever who that is.'

'The man who stands accused of the murder of George Frankham.'

He shook his head and shrugged.

'It has been in the newspapers.'

Lord Beckham waived his hand dismissively. 'I have no time for newspapers. When today's news becomes history, then perhaps I shall peruse it. Not before. But — murder, you say?'

'Yes, the man's body was found floating in the Great Bath.'

'Oho, now you intrigue me! What did you say your name was?'

'I didn't. I am Mrs. Amelia Watson, from

London.'

'The only Watson I know of in London is the one who writes about Sherlock Holmes.'

Of course; it stood to reason that a recluse who has created his own gothic realm out of the eyes of the world would still know of Sherlock Holmes. If Mr. Wells' Martians actually were to come to earth, I've no doubt they would arrive holding copies of *The Strand Magazine*. 'He is my husband,' I sighed.

'Really!' Lord Beckham cried, rushing toward me and extending a hand. 'I have read them all and find them fascinating. Contrived, to be sure, but so entertaining! In that case, you must stay for dinner.'

I attempted to demur, but his lordship would have none of it. He crossed back to his desk, picked up the receiver of a small telephone, and barked into it: 'Mrs. Blethyn, there will be a guest for dinner this evening, see to everything, will you ... that is what I said, a guest for dinner, do not argue with me.' Then he set it back down.

Since I had to dine *somewhere* this evening, I reasoned that I could do worse than staying here at the abbey.

'You must tell me more about your husband and Mr. Holmes at dinner,' Lord Beckham went on. 'But first, you must answer one question for me.'

'Yes, my lord?'

'Why in blazes did you make your way here in the first place? Surely you heard the rumours about me.'

'I did, my lord; but, well, I could hardly bring myself to believe them.'

He looked disappointed. 'Really? Blast. Perhaps I have made them too preposterous.'

'You have created the rumours about yourself?'

'In a sense, though it was really more a case of augmenting what was already being said about me,' he responded. 'I had long wanted to live in a gothic edifice like this, and, finding none that suited me, I decided to build my own. Land here was plentiful, not to mention inexpensive, and I supposed that living in the country would remove me from the current civilisation enough that I might be able to study the more important past ones in peace. However, no sooner had the abbey risen from the dust when people began to appear at the door — trying to find out who I was, what I was doing; and even, on occasion, whether I would contribute to a church fete. Can you imagine! A church fete!

'So, I set about scaring the fools away with wild tales of terrible deeds taking place in the dark of the night, all that sort of rubbish. It has been quite effective. Now then, I have answered your question, but you have not answered mine. Why have you come here?'

'I came to consult you regarding that medallion. I was told that you were an expert on ancient cultures.'

'And so I am.' He held up the medallion. 'Where did you get this?'

'Ronald Standish dug it up out of the ground. Have you seen anything like it before?'

'Seen, no. I daresay no one alive has *seen* it — except, of course, for you, me, and your friend the murderer.'

'He is innocent, my lord.'

'Is he? How dull. Do you know who this medallion represents, Mrs. Watson?'

'Finding that out is why I am here.'

'This, my dear lady, is Cam, a Celtic water god, quite popular in this area because of both the springs and the river. Quite a powerful god, too. Cam is the father of Sulis, whose sacred springs were what we now call the baths. The Romans, of course, later corrupted Sulis by associating her with one of their own goddesses, Minerva.'

'Like the cat,' I muttered.

'Not cat, dear lady, Cam.'

'Yes, of course. But is that medallion valuable enough to kill someone over?'

'Oh, gods, yes!' he replied emphatically. 'Ignoring its worth in gold, which is the least of its values, this is an important artefact of a powerful religion. It is no less important a find than if, say, the Mandylion of Edessa had been discovered.'

'The what?'

'The Mandylion of Edessa, a small cloth reputed to hold the miraculous image of the face of Yehoshua the Anointed, which disappeared from Constantinople in the thirteenth century.'

Lord Beckham spoke so rapidly and precisely, like a skilfully-played harpsichord, that it took a great deal of concentration to keep up with him. 'I'm sorry,' I said, 'Ye-ho-shua the Anointed?'

'Better known as Jesus Christ, thanks to ancient Greek translators who rendered the Hebrew name 'Yehoshua' as 'Jesus', and the term 'messiah' — 'the anointed one' — as 'christos'. I try to refer to all deities, even the minor ones, by their correct names, and I assure you that if Yehoshua the Anointed were to suddenly materialise here in this room and you were to blurt out 'Jesus Christ', he would have no more idea that you were addressing him than if you had said 'Lord Nelson'. Your friend found this, you say?'

I launched into a recounting of the death of George Frankham and the case against Ronnie Standish, and my suspicion that the medallion had something to do with the killing.

'So you are saying this Ronnie person killed his employer for this medallion?'

'No! I have told you I believe Ronnie to be innocent.'

'Hm,' he mused. 'If devotion to a god, any god, did not result in bloodshed, that would certainly be a first.'

I was about to argue the point when the tiny butler re-entered the room. 'My lord, Lynds requests your presence in the carriage house,' he said. 'He wants you to inspect the work he has done on the new vehicle.'

'Oh, yes, of course,' Lord Beckham said, his attention so diverted by the request that he appeared to all but forget the medallion, which he started to slip into his jacket pocket as he headed for the door.

'My lord,' I said, 'technically that medallion is not yours to keep.'

'What? Oh, yes, I suppose not. Right you are, though I would very much like to study it further.' He stepped back to his desk, opened a door and dropped the medallion in, then shut it and locked it, taking the key. 'It shall be safe in here until I return, then you may take it when you leave. Edgar, please show Mrs. Watson to the Regal Room. She is staying for dinner.'

'She is what?' the dwarf, apparently named Edgar, asked incredulously.

'She is staying for dinner, you little homunculus, and don't act so shocked, there is a first time for everything!' Then, turning to me, he added: 'Should there be anything you require, please let Edgar know. Dinner is promptly at six — I believe in dining early. Enjoy yourself, dear lady.' With that, he strode out of the room.

'Your master is quite an interesting man,' I commented weakly to the servant.

'And if I may say so, madam, you must be quite an interesting woman,' Edgar replied. 'Never before has anyone been asked to stay for dinner. Please come this way.'

The Regal Room was on the second floor, near the top of a decadently wide staircase. Outside the room, as though guarding it, stood a full suit of armour, complete with a lance. Once inside, it was easy to see how the room had received its designation: everything inside from the bed curtains to the carpet to the walls to the bindings of the books in a glass-fronted bookcase was one shade or other of purple, the regal colour of tradition.

One wall sported a copy of Gainsborough's painting *The Blue Boy*, which was perfectly executed except for the fact that the placid young man now wore a lavender satin suit. Until that moment, I had not realised there were so many variations of the colour purple.

'I hope you will be comfortable here, madam,' Edgar said.

In truth, I suspected I would soon begin to feel like I had found myself inside a grape, but I thanked him and he took his leave. On the wall opposite the four-poster bed was a large stone fireplace — painted purple, of course — and while it presently contained no blaze, I could not help but wonder how his lordship forced the logs to produce purple flames.

Seating myself in a large, and very comfortable, purple chair, I reviewed in my mind everything I had learned in the last two days about Ronald Standish's predicament, and no matter from which direction I approached the central problem, the conclusion remained the same: the young man was in almost intractable trouble. I was not, of course, ready to pronounce Ronnie guilty, but I could not honestly see any way in which he could prove his innocence under the weight of the evidence, without a sudden confession from a third party. I only hoped Geoffrey Creach was having more success on that front.

When my eyes became overflowing with purple, I turned to the window and gazed out at the blessedly verdant grounds, which seemed to roll on as far as the eye could see. The view from the top of the abbey's tower must be truly breathtaking. I was suddenly struck by the urge to find out.

Stepping to the long purple bell cord that dangled beside the bed, I gave it a tug and waited. In hardly any time at all, there was a knock on the door. 'Come in,' I said, and Edgar appeared.

'Yes, madam?'

'Edgar, it is still a few hours until dinner, and I was wondering if it might be possible for me to see a little more of this unique house, particularly the tower. Is it accessible?'

'Completely,' the little man answered, 'though there are quite a number of steps to the top.'

I assured him it would be no problem, and he obligingly led me through more of the incredible house, past literally dozens of glass display cases, each containing rows of what appeared to be artefacts from earlier civilizations, only the most obvious of which — such as an exquisite Egyptian cat — I could identify. Most intriguing were a pair of graceful marble arms that would, by my estimation, have fit precisely onto the Venus de Milo. How he came into possession of all these objects I could only guess.

Finally, we came to what appeared to be the entrance to a cave, hewn out of stone. It was plaster, of course, but artfully done. Through the 'cave' entrance was the beginning of a spiral staircase.

'Follow it up to the lantern,' Edgar said. 'Should you have any problems, simply come back down, or use the telephone at the top and I shall come to get you.'

'I am sure I will be fine, thank you.'

Halfway up the stairs, I reassessed my prediction. I had not taken into account the toll that bicycling from Bath to the countryside would take on my legs, which were beginning to feel like molten lead. Still I continued to climb (this had, after all, been my idea), and it was not long until I came to the 'lantern' — a hexagonal chamber at the top completely enclosed by glass, save for one solid door through which one could escape outside onto the small walkway that encircled it, the rail of which held several large rooks.

The view was indeed breathtaking. Green land and forest rolled out on all sides, occasionally quilted by patches of field; a greater expanse of land than I believe I had ever seen. To the south, one could see the outline of Bath, though from the distance the stone buildings formed together into dark shapes, making the city look somewhat like an ancient stone circle amidst the green.

But as I was enjoying the view (and the lack of purple), a horrible sound suddenly intruded upon the tranquillity; a monstrous roaring followed by what sounded like gunfire. The source of the sound was not evident, even from this vantage point, and I could not help but wonder if there was a lumber mill in proximity. After a few moments the sound vanished as quickly as it had started. It was most curious. Turning my gaze once more to the shadow of Bath, I was suddenly struck by the notion that somewhere walking around in that city, invisible to me here in the tower, was the killer of George Frankham.

If I only knew where to look.

At the first sign of waning daylight I headed back down the tower steps (an easier task than ascending them), and returned to the Regal Room, where someone — presumably Edgar — had thoughtfully delivered a full teapot. At six o'clock sharp I left the purple room (which in the waning light appeared to ripen and bruise) and descended to the entrance hall. The tiny manservant escorted me to the dinner.

Compared to the rest of the house, the dining room was shockingly small, with a table that in size would have suited the downstairs kitchen of any London townhouse. Then again, it had been made clear that a dinner invitation from Lord Beckham was rarer than the appearance of Halley's Comet. I took a seat at the table, and waited for his lordship, who emerged only moments later, elegantly dressed for dinner in white tie and tails. It even looked as though he had tamed his hair somewhat, and possibly trimmed his white beard.

As soon as he was seated Edgar delivered bowls of what smelled like an excellent turtle soup. One taste verified the judgment.

'This is wonderful,' I said.

'Mrs. Blethyn is the finest cook in Europe,' he acknowledged. 'Wait until the game hen arrives. I had a chance to look more at that gold medallion you brought, by the way.'

'And did you discover anything more about it?'

'Nothing beyond my initial judgment, that it is negative first-, possibly negative second-century Celtic.'

'You mean second-century B.C.?'

'A totally worthless term,' his lordship sneered, spooning up a mouthful of soup. 'A more useful term would be 'B.C.A.' — 'Before the Common Age' — or something of that sort. Dating history from the birth of our friend Yehoshua, who was during his lifetime just another prophet who ran afoul of the authorities, is a fluke of monumental proportions.'

'Some, my lord, might say that you speak heresy.'

'I speak it without an accent, Mrs. Watson. In fact, in another time, I would likely be burned at the stake on the abbey green.'

'You sound almost pleased with the

thought.'

I caught a twinkle in his eye as he said: 'If you knew what was required to heat a house of this size in the winter, you would not turn down the promise of free warmth, no matter how it was offered.'

The game hen then arrived, and I took a bite of the tender, delicately-spiced meat. 'I agree with you totally, Lord Beckham,' I said.

'About my burning at the stake?'

'No, about Mrs. Blethyn. This is wonderful.' We dined in silence for a bit, then I posed: 'Your words imply a certain disdain for Christianity. Are you an atheist?'

He set down his silverware with a *plunk*. 'Now you disappoint me, dear lady. That is precisely the sort of ignorant prejudice that I try to shut out of my doors and frighten away — this notion that one must either be a Christian or an atheist. The truth is, I am neither. I believe in the validity of all deities, and their existence as well.'

'You can't mean that.'

'Oh, but I do. No god or goddess in any religion exists in and of itself, at least not the way that you or I exist, as a being that can be touched, seen, heard or, depending on the being, smelled. Rather, they draw their existence, indeed their power, from the people who believe in them, and the more belief that is generated, the more powerful the deity becomes. Might through numbers, if you will.'

'Why, then, has Christianity flourished and survived for thousands of years? Are you saying it is simply luck?'

'Oh no, dear lady, not luck. Power. Why does the Church of England worship a modified form of Yahweh rather than Jupiter, or Enlil, or Ahura Mazda — or Cam, for that matter? Because sixteen centuries ago the Roman Emperor Constantine, the most powerful man in the known world at that time, gave his subjects a choice: to either accept a local fledgling faith called Christianity as the state religion, or perish. Not wishing to perish, they accepted, rejecting all other gods.'

'To think what Mr. Darwin would make of this theory!'

'Ha, ha! Very good, madam! But, unlike living corporeal creatures, gods do not face extinction as fitter ones survive. Oh, they fall out of popularity, perhaps, but as long as their power has been invested in a site, a building — even an object — a vestige of them remains.'

'An object like that medallion?'

'Precisely. If its power can be unlocked by worshippers, the god is awakened.'

'But surely worshippers of Cam no longer exist.'

'Why do you say that?' he snapped.

'Well ... because it is an old god.'

'Yahweh has probably existed for a longer time in human history, yet he has no shortage of supporters.'

'Do you know of any contemporary Cam worshippers?'

After sucking the meat off a hen bone, he regarded me with amusement. 'What you really want to know is whether I am a Cam worshipper.'

'You do know quite a bit about him.'

'I do indeed, but I thought I had already made it clear that I am a scholar in such matters, not a practitioner. If you ask me, do I believe in Cam, the answer is yes, because I believe in all gods. However, dancing around in an oak grove and prostrating myself before the old fish-face is another thing altogether.'

A light, delicious dessert of cream and cherries followed the meal, after which I realised that I had best be getting back to the hotel, and I made mention of such to his lordship, only to receive a startling reply.

'Oh, it is too much to expect you to navigate the green on a bicycle at this time of night,' he said. 'You must spend the night here and return tomorrow.'

'Really, Lord Beckham, I hardly think that is seemly.'

'My good woman, I assure you I am not some 'Uncle Silas' from a wretched novel, luring you here for dark and demented purposes. I am offering you the comfort of my home because travelling through the dark by bicycle, particularly for one largely unfamiliar with the local environs, would be both difficult and dangerous.'

'Perhaps you might avail me of a coach and coachman?' I asked politely.

'It is in dire need of repair, I am afraid.'

'Oh? Did I not hear Edgar mention a new vehicle earlier tonight?'

Lord Beckham's eyes sparkled. 'Oh-ho,

the new vehicle! Yes, we might be able to arrange something for you at that.' He rang for the servant, who only moments before had stepped out with the dessert plates. When the placid little man had returned, his lordship said: 'Edgar, please have Lynds bring the new vehicle up to the house. I shall take the reins myself.'

I admit that I was puzzled by this, since he had just said his carriage was in need of repair.

Rising from the table, Lord Beckham said, 'It will only take a moment, then we shall take our leave, Mrs. Watson.'

'Um, my lord, aren't you forgetting something?'

'Am I?'

'The medallion?'

'Ah, yes, you are right. Let me get it for you.' He dashed into his study and re-emerged momentarily holding the golden object and a sheet of paper. 'I took the liberty of making a detailed sketch of it for further research purposes. It hardly does it justice, though.' As he handed the medallion to me, I caught sight of the drawings he had made. Far from doing it ill justice, he had so expertly rendered both the front and back of the disc in pencil that at first it appeared to be a photograph. I was about to compliment him on his skill as a sketch artist when a detail from the back view drawing caught my attention, and I gasped.

'Is something amiss?' he asked, as I continued to stare at the drawing.

'What is that?' I managed to say, pointing to a marking on the back of the medallion that looked something like a fish.

'It is etched into the back of the medallion, though very lightly, so much so that I almost overlooked it. I darkened it for the sake of the drawing.'

Dropping the paper, I held up the medallion to the light and looked at the back. I had completely overlooked it too, but now, very faintly, I could see the mark. 'What does it signify?' I asked, breathlessly.

'In practical terms, it signifies the authenticity of the medallion,' he replied. 'That is the symbol of a worshipper of Cam. It is how they identified themselves.'

'I see,' I uttered absently, continuing to stare at the mark etched into the back of the medallion — a mark that was identical to the strange monogram that I had noticed on the shirt of George Frankham's that Ronnie Standish had been wearing.

7

Could George Frankham have been a modern worshipper of the ancient god Cam? Could that have had anything to do with the reason he was killed? 'Of course it could have,' I muttered aloud.

'What's that?' his lordship asked.

'Oh, I'm sorry, I was just thinking.' I tucked the medallion safely into my handbag.

'Admirable as that may be, we must be on our way if we are to go to the city.'

As we stepped out of the abbey into the night, I was startled by that same horrific sound I had heard in the tower — only now it was getting closer! 'What in heaven's name is that?' I demanded. My mouth fell open as a liveried man wearing eye goggles — presumably Lynds the coachman — drove up to the front of the house in a bright green motorcar!

'What do you think?' Lord Beckham shouted over the noise of the engine. 'It is a Vulcan Two-seater Runabout with a three-cylinder engine specially calibrated to achieve twenty horsepower.'

To me it looked like a shaking, smoking bathtub fastened behind a fireplace grate, draped with two lanterns and set atop pram wheels. The man Lynds pulled a handbrake and shut off the engine, then clambered out of the contraption, stripped the goggles off his face and handed them to Lord Beckham.

'There is a pair in here for you, too, Mrs. Watson,' his lordship said. Then, turning to Lynds, he commanded: 'See if you can get that bicycle over there into the back seat.'

'Lord Beckham, I don't think ... I mean, perhaps simply taking the bicycle back would be best.'

'No, no, it won't do. I'm afraid your only choice is stay at the abbey until daylight then pedal back, or ride with me into town tonight.'

I could see an opportunity for catastrophe either way, though I had to admit that while I have seen bicyclists upended and injured, I have never seen a motorcar in a similar situation. It was only those trying to walk around them that were in danger. 'Very well, my lord,' I sighed, 'I shall go with you.'

'Capital!' he cried, climbing in behind the steering wheel on the left side, while Lynds managed to secure the bicycle in the cart-like space in the rear. Gingerly I climbed in beside Lord Beckham, removed my hat, and attempted to get the goggles over my hair. I no sooner had them in place than the vehicle suddenly lurched forward and we sped down the carriage drive.

Holding my hat with one hand, I clutched onto the rail that ran beside the seat with the other and braved the wind that rushed past us. The twin lanterns on the front illuminated only so far in front of us, and I was developing a dreadful fear that if a stag or some other large animal happened out of the woods in front of us, we would not see it in time to avoid a collision. Fortunately, we saw no wildlife as we bounced and chugged through the trees and out onto the green, and then to the Old Road. Once on the larger road, Lord Beckham shouted: 'Now we'll really see what she's made of!' The motorcar lurched forward again and proceeded down the road like a runaway horse.

'How fast does this go?' I asked.

'I'm told it could cover a distance of thirty miles in an hour!' Lord Beckham answered.

'Dear God,' I muttered, not caring which one ... might they all protect me!

The distance I had taken a good half-hour by bicycle ground underneath the wheels of the motorcar in a fraction of that time, and before long we had come to the edge of the city. In front of us was a horse cart, and Lord Beckham responded to its presence by tooting a large, curved horn attached to the car and shouting: 'Out of the way!' As the motorcar blazed past, the horse reared in terror, while the driver tried desperately to keep control of the cart. 'Horses are for the last century!' his lordship declared. 'They should keep them off the streets!'

How one person could be so obsessed with the past that he felt compelled to painstakingly create a house that looked like an ancient, crumbling ruin, and not care about current events until they became past history ... and yet throw all caution aside and embrace every modern invention, was a conundrum even Mr. Holmes could not have unravelled.

As we sped towards the centre of the city and the abbey, the number of people and horses on the street became more plentiful, as did the shouts of his lordship. Believing the best course of action was to not watch, I tightly shut my eyes behind the goggles and held on as the motorcar veered and careened from side to side, up- and down-hill, until it finally came to rest. Cracking open one eye, I saw that we were in front of the Roman Hotel. Mrs. Grimes, no doubt alarmed by the din of the motorcar, peered through the front window.

Lord Beckham, meanwhile, leapt out and wrestled the bicycle out of the Vulcan Two-seater Runabout. 'I enjoyed our chat, Mrs. Watson,' he said. 'Tell the owner of that medallion that if he ever does decide to sell it, I am interested.'

'I shall,' I replied, shakily. Then something struck me, a bit of our earlier conversation. 'Before you go, my lord, I have one last question.'

'Mmmm?'

'You described the Cam worshippers as dancing around in an oak grove.'

'I did.'

'Well, my lord, if you are not a member of the congregation yourself, how do you know they meet in an oak grove?'

He raised his goggles and steadied his gaze on me. Uncharacteristically slowly, he said: 'Mrs. Watson, if you had spent as much time as I have studying Celtic religions, you would know that the Celts considered oak groves to be the kind of sacred places of which I spoke earlier. It is the logical place for such a ritual.'

'I understand, my lord.'

He continued to look at me, his mind un-readable through his face. 'Do you really?' he finally said. Then, pushing the goggles back down over his eyes, he leapt back into the driver's seat and threw the motorcar into action and pulled away. It lurched and spluttered down the street and disappeared around the corner.

If this was really an example of a quiet provincial English town, I had best stay in London. Staggering up the porch to the front door, I knocked on the door and waited for Mrs. Grimes to open it, which she did on the second knock.

''Tis a good thing you're back,' she said in hushed tones. '*Himself* is here.'

'Himself?' I said, entering the hotel, still vibrating from the motorcar ride. 'Himself who?'

'Himself I,' a familiar voice responded from behind me.

Turning, I saw my husband standing there, and in our three years together, I do not believe I had ever seen him looking quite so displeased.

'John ... what a surprise,' I said, weakly.

'The surprise is all mine, I assure you.'

'Well ... how nice to see you.'

'I have been waiting for you for the better part of two hours, Amelia!'

''Tis alone I'll leave you two lovebirds,' Mrs. Grimes said, practically running out of the room.

When she was gone (but most likely not out of earshot) I said: 'I'm sorry, John, but I was not expecting you. In fact, aren't you supposed to be in Scotland?'

'The engagement fell through,' he said in an agitated manner. 'As soon as I got to Glasgow I learned that the man I was to replace was not sick at all, just feigning illness as a way of bettering his contract. The nerve of some people!'

'I'm so sorry, darling, but why have you come here?'

'Well, *darling*,' he said, rather pointedly, 'I got back to London this morning to find you and Missy gone and the telephone ringing. It was a reporter from the *Police Gazette* asking for a comment about the murder investigation that you were conducting in Bath!'

Mr. Bryce, I thought.

'I had no idea what he was talking about, but I jumped on the next train down here to find out what you were doing. Where *is* Missy, by the way?'

'At the house of an old friend. John, I am here to try and help an old student whose husband is accused of murder.'

'You are here working on a murder case?'

'Well, she wrote me a letter and —'

'And you could not have bothered to leave a note for me as to your whereabouts?' he cried. 'Holmes at least included me in his plans!'

'John, I fully expected to be back before you returned from Scotland.'

'Unless you managed to get yourself murdered, gallivanting off to God knows where playing detective!'

Now it was my turn to bristle. 'Do you know how many nights I have thought the same thing about you?' I demanded. 'With no warning, the game's afoot and you grab your service revolver and run off with your pre-wife Sherlock Holmes to hide in a bush somewhere and wait to be shot at!'

John opened his mouth to reply, but no sound came out. Finally he closed it and a slight, sad smile formed on his lips. 'What a pair we are, aren't we, Amelia?'

Oh, that smile; oh, those hearth-warm brown eyes. 'What a team we are, darling.'

'Can you forgive me?' we both said in unison.

The answer was clearly *yes*, since the forgiving commenced not five minutes later up in my room at the Roman Hotel. The details are no one's business but John's and mine.

Suffice it to say we awoke late the next morning, having made the best of a small bed.

Mrs. Grimes rapped on the door shortly after nine, at which time we were not quite ready to emerge for the day, though I was able to ask through the door if she would kindly bring a breakfast tray to the room. When she came back, John and I had finished dressing.

'Here you are, ma'am, sir,' she said, smiling, handing us the tray filled with eggs, ham, bread and a pot of tea.

'Thank you, Mrs. Grimes,' John said. 'And since I was rather distracted and not at my best last night, let me say now that your hospitality is excellent.'

''Tis thankin' you I am, sir,' she said, grinning broadly. 'Let me know if you'll be needin' anything else.'

We closed the door behind her and attended to our breakfast, while I tried as best I could to fill John in on what had transpired since coming to Bath, focusing on the matter of the medallion and what I had discovered at the home of Lord Beckham. I retrieved my handbag and pulled it out to show it to him, but as I did, two slips of paper that had been caught in the chain came with it and fluttered to the floor. I picked them up and set them on the bed while John hefted the medallion.

'So you believe this Frankham fellow was part of some strange religious cult, and that is why he was killed?' he asked. 'Or was he killed because of this medallion?'

'I am not certain yet,' I replied. 'The truth is, I am quite at a loss. I do not want to believe that the medallion was the direct motive for the murder, because if it were, the implication for the killing would lie with the person holding possession of it.'

'In other words, Standish.'

'Yes. There has to be something I'm missing, John. There has to be another motive for the murder.' As I bowed my head in thought, my attention had suddenly and irrevocably been captured by the two slips of paper that had fallen from my handbag, which I had set on the bed. One was the business card from the photographer's shop I had visited yesterday, and the other was the slip of photograph that I had retrieved from the smashed frame in the home of George Frankham.

'Oh,' I muttered, looking at the fragments, 'oh dear.' I edged the sliver of photographic paper over the top of the card and said, 'Oh,' again.

'I know that 'oh',' John said. 'Something has come to you, hasn't it?'

I held up the slip of photographic paper with the mysterious letters on them for John to see. 'Inside the home of George Frankham was a picture frame that someone had smashed and clumsily attempted to hide in the fireplace. Whoever it was had torn out the photograph but in their haste left this corner of it. There were words scrawled on the back.'

'*Ice ... her ... lest,*' John read. 'Obviously the remnants of a message, but there is not enough left of it to decipher.'

'Not a message, John, a name and address.' I handed him the photographer's business card that I had acquired earlier, which read: *J. Allardice, Photographer, Argyle Street.* 'Do you see it? Take the last three letters from 'Allardice', the last three from 'Photographer' —'

'And the last two from 'Argyle' combined with 'St', the abbreviation for 'Street',' he said, nodding. 'And you have what appears to be 'ice, her, lest'. All well and good, but what does it mean?'

'It means that the photograph that was torn out of the frame in George Frankham's home came from the studio of J. Allardice, whom I happened to meet yesterday. It means that he may know what was in that photograph that someone, presumably the killer, was in such a hurry to destroy. Come, John, we must see Mr. Allardice at once.'

'What we should really do is take this to the local police,' John said.

'If we did that, dear, I would be forced to tell that brute of an inspector how I obtained this sliver of paper, what I was doing inside the house of George Frankham, and who else was there with me. Having revealed all that, I have no doubt that the man would throw me into the town gaol for withholding evidence.'

My husband sighed. 'Sometimes I wonder why cannot you stay at home and tat doilies like other men's wives, instead of diving headlong into trouble.'

'Just as I sometimes wonder why you cannot dispense pills and set bones like other doctors, instead of carrying the banner of Sherlock Holmes across the kingdom like Richard the Lionheart on a crusade. Now, finish your breakfast, and let us go see Mr. Allardice.'

Three-quarters of an hour later, we arrived in front of the shop of J. Allardice; and, trying the door, I found it to be open. Walking in, I called, 'Hello, Mr. Allardice?' but received no reply. The waiting area consisted of a counter with a curtain backing, and a few photographs hung up on the walls for decoration or promotion. 'Mr. Allardice?' I called again, and again received only silence in response. 'Perhaps he stepped out.'

'Or is in the back,' John said, heading for the curtained back room. A few seconds after he disappeared behind the curtain, I heard him utter: 'Great Scott!'

'What is it?' I called, rushing behind the counter and through the doorway that the curtain covered. In the dim light I could make out a shape on the floor, which upon closer inspection proved to be the man I had spoken briefly with yesterday. John was kneeling over the body, examining him. 'He is dead,' he said, quietly. 'He has been bludgeoned. And look at this studio.'

Shelves of photographic equipment, paper and jars of chemicals had been knocked to the floor, as though a titanic struggle had taken place here. Yet the fact that several file-cabinet drawers hung open with their contents in disarray argued more that whomever had killed Mr. Allardice had also been engaged in a hunt. 'What do you suppose they were looking for?' I asked.

'Most likely the same thing we are,' John said, 'evidence that indicated whatever was in that mysterious picture frame you discovered. Let's see if we cannot get some light in here.' John began searching the walls for a light switch; upon finding one, he turned it, and instantly the room was bathed in an eerie red glow, which did not help our search much. Stepping to a high window, John pulled back the curtains and let the sunlight in, diffusing the red rays and making the blood on the unfortunate Mr. Allardice's forehead become more visible.

'John, look at his hand. It appears he is holding something.'

Forcing open the fingers of J. Allardice's hand, John found an object inside, and held it up for me to see.

It was a button, about the size of a tuppence, dark brown with yellow edging.

Glancing over the man's clothing, I could find no button that matched it. 'Where do you suppose that came from?'

'If I had to put forth a guess, I would say that it came off during the struggle with his killer.' Then something else caught his attention. 'What have we over here?' he asked, stepping to a table that held bottles of chemicals, most of them overturned, and crouching to look underneath it.

'What do you see?'

'Look underneath the table. A jar of some liquid has been spilled and it has left a most peculiar stain.' I followed his direction and saw what was indeed a strange spillage: the top edges of the still-damp stain in question were straight and perpendicular, a situation that could not occur naturally. John bent down and examined the spot. 'There is a trap door of some kind here,' he said. 'The liquid fell through the cracks, and that is why the surrounding stain appears to have sharp edges.' He looked around until he found a knife, which he used to pry the trap open.

'Is anything inside?' I asked.

John did not answer, but merely reached in and pulled out a black satchel that was damp from the spilled chemicals. Opening it up, he pulled out a bundle of white satiny material, which he held up and shook out. Stitched into the front, roughly over where the wearer's heart would be, was the fish-like symbol of Cam.

'What do you suppose this is?' he asked.

'A robe worn by a worshipper of Cam during secret ceremonies.'

'Are you certain?'

'Look at this mark,' I said, pointing out the fish icon. 'Lord Beckham, who is an expert in such things, identified it as the sign of a worshipper.'

'So this means Allardice was also part of this cult,' he said.

'So it would seem. Why else would he have such a garment? Why else would he endeavour to keep it hidden?'

Tossing aside the robe, John reached back into the satchel, this time withdrawing two photographic plates. 'Ah, now perhaps we have something that will explain the killings,' he said. He held the first one up to the light for both of us to see, but there was nothing visible on it, only a series of white lines and scratches on a dark surface. The second plate revealed more: it was a reverse image of a photograph, which made it difficult to make out, but it was clearly a study of a man, and he appeared to be wearing a robe, but not like the one we had just found. This robe was light in negative, which meant in the photograph it would have appeared dark, not white. What struck me, though, was the object the man held in his hands. Exactly what it was could not be discerned, but even in negative I could make out a bearded fish-like face, similar to the one on the medallion.

'Could the man in this photograph be Frankham?' John asked.

I squinted at the plate. 'I cannot tell. I have only really seen him from a painting.'

'I wish I knew how to use this equipment. Only seeing a photographic print will tell us anything.'

At that moment a noise came from beyond the curtain. 'John, did you hear that?' I whispered. He did not answer, but held his finger to his lips and stepped back into the shadows. More noise followed; someone had entered the shop, and a voice was barking out commands. My heart fell as I recognised the voice. A moment later, the curtain was pulled aside and an electric torch was thrust through the doorway, followed by a police constable.

'Blimey!' he hollered. 'There's a dead man here!'

Before long another man was in the doorway, and we stood frozen while the torch slowly rose over us.

'Well, well, well, look what we have here,' the coarse voice said. 'Didn't I warn you to stay out of my way, or am I getting forgetful?'

With a sinking heart, I looked into the maliciously grinning face of Inspector James McCallum.

'Darling,' I sighed, 'this is Inspector McCallum, head of the local constabulary. Inspector, this is my husband, Dr. John Watson.'

'Er, Amelia has spoken of you, sir,' John said, holding out his hand.

The boulder-headed policeman merely looked at it with a faint expression of disgust. 'Yes, and I've heard about you, too. You're the lapdog of Sherlock Holmes.'

'Lapdog?' John protested. 'Now, see here — '

'No, you see here!' the inspector shouted. 'I've got a dead body on the floor in there, and the two of you are hiding back here. That's enough for me to make a pinch as far as I'm concerned.'

'Oh, don't be absurd,' John said. 'We did not kill the man.'

'Then what are you doing here?'

I jumped in: 'We came to visit Mr. Allardice and no one answered our call, but the door was open so we came back here and found him like this. My husband is a doctor, so he examined him. We were about to leave and call you when you arrived.'

'Were you now?' the inspector sneered. 'I don't suppose the thought of sneaking out the back ever occurred to you for a moment.'

John bristled. 'I can't say as I like your implication, my good man.'

'Maybe you'd like it better down at the station.'

'Why did you come here, Inspector?' I

asked. 'Did you have an appointment for a sitting?'

He turned to me and glared. 'Don't get funny with me, woman.'

I could feel John tensing next to me and I put a hand on his arm, hoping to calm him down.

'Why'd I come here, you want to know?' the inspector began. 'This bloke's landlady contacted us and he never came home last night. She was worried about him, so I decided to check his place of work. Now that I've told you why I'm here, it's your turn. What caused you to come pay a visit?'

I sensed that further prevarication was useless. I would have to tell the police everything that I had done since arriving in Bath.

'Very well, Inspector,' I said. 'Let us go to the police station and I will tell you whatever you wish to know. But I do want Geoffrey Creach to be present.'

'Solicitor, huh?' McCallum sneered. 'So it's to be a confession, is it?'

'A confession that I have foolishly waded in far over my head. Incidentally, Inspector, you might want to take that black bag, that white robe, and the photographic plates that my husband is holding. They could be evidence.'

The frown on the face of the inspector stayed there for the most part until we arrived at the city's police headquarters. John and I were escorted to Inspector McCallum's office and we sat there in silence, being offered nothing in the way of hospitality, not so much as a glass of water, until the solicitor could be sent for, as I had requested.

Some fifteen minutes later, an aggravated-looking Geoffrey Creach entered, escorted by a constable.

'Inspector,' Mr. Creach said, 'I was told by this man to drop everything and come here at once.' Then he noticed me sitting in the chair. 'What is this about? Have you found Standish?'

'No, we haven't found Standish!' the inspector roared.

'Mr. Creach,' I said, 'I asked that you be here before I gave certain information to the inspector.'

'Information?'

'Yes, it seems that my husband and I

— oh, do forgive me, this is my husband, Dr. John Watson. John, this Geoffrey Creach.'

'A privilege to meet you, Dr. Watson,' he said, nodding. 'But I still do not know what this is about.'

'I think it is time that I informed the inspector about my activities over the last few days. I wanted you to be here as well. The first pertinent clue was finding that discarded picture frame with the sliver of a photograph in the home of Mr. Frankham, and —'

'Hold up!' the inspector interrupted. 'What were you doing inside Frankham's house?'

'Looking for clues, obviously.' Risky though it might be, I was not yet ready to disclose that Ronnie Standish was hiding out there.

'That's it! That's all I need to hear to put you in the lock-up. Maybe breaking and entering isn't a crime in London, but here it is! You've done it now, lady!'

'Not so fast, Inspector,' Mr. Creach said. 'You cannot make a charge of breaking and entering stick unless it is pressed by the owner of the house, who happens to be deceased.'

'I'll press the bloody charge myself!'

'On what grounds?'

'Disregarding a police order!'

'What kind of order? No cordon has been established around the house. No sign has been anywhere on the building warning against trespassing. A person can only disobey orders when those orders are made known. Did you at any point deliberately order Mrs. Watson not to visit and enter the house?'

For a moment I thought the inspector's head was about to explode from within. At its peak of colour (which would have gone nicely in Lord Beckham's Regal Room) he shrieked: 'Quinlan!' Within seconds, an apprehensive looking sergeant scuttled into the room. 'Go to the Frankham house and put up some kind of bloody damn warning sign! Put up ropes! Put up whatever it takes to let people know to stay the hell out, and do it today!'

'Yes sir,' Sergeant Quinlan said before scurrying back out. I felt a cold nervousness as I hoped that Bella and Ronnie would take care not to be seen while the police were out there.

'All right, lady, go on,' the inspector said, looking somewhat defeated.

I told him of my meeting with Mr. Dawes the librarian and of briefly meeting Mr. Allardice and receiving his card, then of the visit to see Lord Beckham.

'You actually spoke with his lordship?' Mr. Creach asked, surprised.

'I had a most stimulating dinner conversation with him and he was quite charming, in a blunt, heretical sort of way,' I replied. 'Perhaps he left his horns with his other suit. Anyway, I went there to learn more about a gold medallion that Ronnie had discovered on Mr. Frankham's property —'

'A gold medallion?' Mr. Creach interrupted. 'I don't recall hearing anything about that.'

'I'm afraid Bella kept that from you. Ronnie had hidden the fact that he discovered it from Mr. Frankham, because he didn't want Mr. Frankham to confiscate it.'

'So that's why he killed him!' Inspector McCallum declared.

'Oh, really, Inspector!' I said. 'If there were a competition in the Olympiad for jumping to conclusions, you would be *wearing* a gold medallion! I do not yet know what part this medallion played, though I am certain it is significant, particularly since there might be a group of people here in the city who worship the image on the medallion, an ancient Celtic water god called Cam.'

'Who do *what*?'

'You cannot be serious, madam,' Mr. Creach said.

'I'm afraid I am, and I believe that Mr. Frankham was part of the group.'

'If anyone is part of such a group, it is Beckham.'

'If so, it is not by admission. I asked him.'

'But you believe this band of pagans to be involved in Frankham's death?'

'I do not know,' I reiterated. 'All I can tell you is what I've pieced together from the evidence. First, there is that empty frame in Mr. Frankham's house. Somebody ripped the photograph out because it revealed something incriminating, or at least uncomfortable. There was a sliver of paper left that held information about the photographer's name and address, which led us to Mr.

Allardice. But when we arrived, we found him dead.'

'Wait, wait,' the solicitor said. 'Allardice is dead? No one's mentioned that!'

'Coshed on the head, it would seem,' John said.

'Just like Frankham,' the inspector chimed in.

'Dear God,' Mr. Creach muttered, and I knew what he was thinking: another body had turned up while Ronnie remained at large.

'If I may continue?' I asked. 'While we were in the photographer's shop John discovered a hidden compartment under the floor that contained this robe bearing the symbol of Cam, the same symbol found on the medallion, and also as a sort of monogram embossed on one of Mr. Frankham's shirts.'

'Oh, now wait just one bleeding minute!' McCallum yelled. 'Just how do you know what was on the victim's shirts?'

'Elementary, Inspector: I saw the shirt when I was inside Mr. Frankham's house.' Before anyone could question that, I went on: 'But, more importantly, that hidden compartment in the floor also contained those two photographic plates. We will not know until we have new photographs struck from them, but my surmise is that one is a photograph of George Frankham. It might even be the very one that was removed from the discarded frame.'

'That is a bit of a leap, isn't it?' Mr. Creach asked.

'What other theory fits the facts?' I replied. 'The house was filled with portraits of Mr. Frankham, so there is every reason to believe that the missing photograph was also of himself, and the fact that it was the only one removed argues that something seen in the picture was somehow dangerous.' I pointed to the photographic plates resting on the inspector's desk. 'The fact that these were hidden also speaks for their danger.'

'Since the photographer's shop had been ransacked,' added John, 'it seems reasonable that whoever did so was searching for these plates recognised their significance.'

'But dangerous to who, and why?' Mr. Creach asked.

'That, I do not know,' I admitted.

'Well I do,' the inspector growled. 'To Standish, who else? He kills Frankham, maybe for a picture, maybe not. Then he kills Allardice, maybe for a picture, maybe not. There isn't one piece of evidence that doesn't point straight to Ronald Bleeding Standish!'

That was when I remembered the button.

'Before you jump to another conclusion, Inspector, there is one more piece of evidence to consider. John, please show him that button we found.'

'Button? Oh, yes, of course.' From his pocket he pulled out the button that had been clenched in Mr. Allardice's hand and set it on the desk. 'The unfortunate photographer was holding this when he died.'

'Ah, now this is real evidence!' Inspector McCallum said, picking it up. 'All I have to do is match this up to Standish's coat, and I've got him for the second murder, too.'

'If, indeed, you can match it,' I said.

'Oh, I'll match it, don't you worry about that. This here's worth a crateful of these things.' The inspector pushed the photographic plates aside.

'You know, Inspector, Mrs. Watson might still be right about these negatives,' Mr. Creach said. 'If you are no longer going to hold them, allow me to take them and have positives struck.'

'You can take them to the devil for all I care,' Inspector McCallum growled.

'You are most kind,' the solicitor said, his voice dripping with sarcasm. Picking the plates up off the desk and stuffing them into his coat pocket: 'May we leave now?'

The inspector made a show of leaning back in this chair, rubbing his jaw with a meaty hand, and looking back and forth at John and me. 'I suppose I haven't got anything to hold you two on, but I'm warning you. Stay out of my way from now on. Go on, get out, the lot of you.'

We did not stand upon niceties. The three of us left without another word. On the street, Mr. Creach said: 'I was struck, Mrs. Watson, by how confident you were in there that the button could not be matched to a jacket of Ronnie's. What do you know?'

'Only that it is an expensive button,' I said, 'and expensive buttons tend to feel at home on expensive clothes, not those worn by tradesmen.'

'I see.' The solicitor hailed a cab. 'I would like to ask you to join me.'

'Where now?'

'To Frankham's house. I am afraid it is time to convince Ronnie to turn himself in.'

'Really, Mr. Creach,' I said, getting in the hansom, followed by John, 'you cannot believe he killed Mr. Allardice.'

The solicitor managed to squeeze in and gave the address to the driver.

'Whether he killed anyone or not,' he declared, 'the safest place for him right now might be in the gaol. If I bring him in, he will have some protection. Now that that ignoramus McCallum has been tipped off about Frankham's house, the police may start searching it, no doubt finding Ronnie in the process. Who knows what might happen to Ronnie if he attempts to flee again?'

'He does have a point, Amelia,' John said.

The cab whisked us to Ashdown Crescent and stopped to let us out in front of the house that, on the outside at least, still looked dark and empty. It was good to see that Ronnie and Bella were being careful. When no one on the street was watching, we snuck through the door in the fence and into the back. Mr. Creach marched up to the rear door and gave what sounded like a coded knock. Then a voice from the other side whispered: 'Mr. Creach?'

'Yes, and I am here with the Watsons. Let us in.'

The door creaked open and we entered the house, which was dark due to all of the curtains being drawn, and illuminated sparsely by candles. Bella greeted us, but instantly turned suspicious upon seeing John, a stranger to her.

'Bella, this is Dr. Watson,' I said, and her entire demeanour changed, becoming sunny and polite.

'Is Ronnie here?' the solicitor asked.

'Upstairs, changing,' Bella said. 'Do you have news?'

'Bella, Ronnie has to go back to the police. The situation has gotten worse.'

'Worse? How can it get worse? He is already suspected of murder!'

'Now he is suspected of two murders.'

Bella sank into a chair. 'What will

become of us?' she muttered.

At that moment Ronnie Standish came down the stairs. 'What is happening?' he asked.

'John, perhaps we should wait in the other room while Mr. Creach speaks to them,' I whispered, and my husband agreed. Taking a candle, we stepped into the living room. How trying it must have been for Bella to live virtually inside of a cave. Pointing out the array of picture frames, I said, 'You see what I meant, darling? These are all of the man himself. This is like the sitting room of Narcissus. You can see the space on the mantle where the missing photograph once stood.'

'Yes, and I can see something else, too,' John said, staring up at the painting. Holding the candle up to the portrait, he picked up a fireplace poker with his other hand and pointed at the painted image of George Frankham's chest.

Then I saw it, too.

'Good heavens,' I uttered, looking at the buttons on the jacket Mr. Frankham was wearing in the painting. Even without a magnifying glass it was plain to see that the button on Mr. Frankham's jacket in the painting — brown, with yellow edging — matched the button John had found.

8

'John,' I moaned, 'please don't try to tell me that Mr. Allardice was murdered by a dead man!'

'Hardly,' my ever-rational husband answered. 'More likely it was someone dressed in Frankham's clothing.'

'Oh, dear. When I first came here with Bella, Ronnie was wearing Mr. Frankham's clothing. That's how I knew about the monogram.'

'That jacket specifically?' he asked, pointing to the painting.

'No, not the jacket, not that I saw, but he admitted to retrieving the clothing from Mr. Frankham's bedroom. He could have taken anything.'

John shook his head. 'I know you are convinced of the lad's innocence, Amelia, but I have to say that if someone were deliberately trying to convict themselves of a crime through circumstantial evidence, they could not possibly do a better job of it.'

'We do not know for certain that he ever wore the jacket.'

'That is easy enough to find out,' he said, setting down the poker and walking back into the hallway of the house.

The scene that greeted us there was to be expected, under the circumstances: Ronnie Standish was angry and defiant about being told he must surrender himself to the police, Bella Standish was distraught and in tears, and Geoffrey Creach was desperately attempting to explain his rationale to the two. Finally, in frustration, the solicitor threw his hands up in the air and turned his back on them. 'Mrs. Watson, could you try to explain it to them?' he asked. 'I am getting nowhere.'

Before I even attempted to, however, John surprised me by crying: 'All right, that's enough!'

The room quieted.

'Neither of you two know me,' John told the young couple, 'not as well as you know my wife, at any rate. So please accept that I have been involved in the solving of crimes for some twenty-five years alongside my friend Sherlock Holmes. One does not spend time in the company of such a man or collaborate in his activities as a consulting detective without learning a thing or two about crime and this country's legal system. If my reputation means anything to you, I would suggest, Standish, that you listen to your solicitor, or else face the gravest of consequences.'

'I cannot go back to that inhuman gaol!' Ronnie cried. 'I must be free!'

'And you really consider *this* freedom?' John asked, gesturing to the room. 'Hiding in the dark, unable to leave, fearing every knock on the door, thinking that this time it might be the police? They will be here before long, incidentally, to cordon off the building.'

'Tell us what to do,' Bella beseeched.

'I thought I had already done so,' John replied. 'Standish must turn himself in.'

'You cannot force me to!'

John softened his stance. 'Quite right, young man, I cannot. Neither can Creach here. Neither can my wife — or your wife, for that matter. All any of us can do is advise about what is best, and beyond that, my boy, it is your decision entirely. While you are weighing your options, there is a question I must ask. Standish, did you appropriate a suit of Frankham's while you were here?'

'A suit? Well, I borrowed a shirt and trousers, and one night while I went outside to take some air I began to get chilled, so I came in and put the jacket on.'

'Go and get it and bring it down here, if you would.'

Ronnie did as he was told, dashing up the stairs and returning seconds later with a brown woollen suit jacket, which he tossed to John. Catching it, John immediately looked at the front, and then held it up for Mr. Creach to see. 'The button that was found in Allardice's dead hand matches these three exactly. Now look at this.' He pointed to a spot where a fourth button had been torn off.

'I don't understand,' Ronnie Standish said.

Mr. Creach sighed. 'Hard evidence now in the hands of the police proves that who-ever killed Allardice was wearing this jacket at the time.'

'That is preposterous! Now you are say-ing that I wore this coat to go out and kill someone I've never met in my life?'

'Can't we simply burn the jacket?' Bella asked.

'Oh, heavens, child, that would make things even worse,' I replied. 'Besides, there is still the painting over the mantel.'

'So that is it,' Mr. Creach said admiringly in John's direction, 'you saw the buttons in the painting and deduced it was Frankham's jacket. Fine work, sir.'

'All right, everybody stop talking, please, and let me think!' Ronnie shouted. 'When did this other man, this Aldress —'

'Allardice,' I corrected.

'Whatever! When was he killed?'

'It had to be sometime last evening since I saw him alive earlier in the day.'

'Fine, good! I swear to all of you that I did not leave this house, dressed in that jacket or otherwise, any time yesterday afternoon or evening. I was here all night. You can ask Bella.'

'He was here,' she concurred. 'Except for one time after we ate dinner, when he went outside for a few minutes.'

'How many minutes?' I asked.

'Fifteen, maybe. I wasn't keeping track.'

'Not long enough to leave and go kill somebody,' Ronnie stated. 'I ... I have to get out into the open sometimes. Even in a house this size the walls begin to close in on me.'

'Did you wear the jacket when you went out?'

'I don't remember.'

'The clothes you are wearing now are your own, are they not?'

'Yes. Bella laundered them for me.'

'So,' John said, 'if everybody is satisfied that Standish never left last night, all we have to do is eliminate the impossible to explain how the button from a coat he had worn came to be in the dead man's hand.'

'Perhaps you put it there,' Ronnie fired back. 'After all, you say you were the one who discovered it. Maybe the button wasn't in his hand at all. Maybe you just pretended to find it there, to make it look like I had killed him! Maybe *you* are the killer, Dr. Watson! I mean, that's just as easy to explain as my doing it, isn't it?'

For a moment I feared John would become angry, having the accusation thrown at him in such a way, but instead his face remained thoughtful for a moment, and then he smiled. 'You know, son, though I hate to admit it, you are quite right,' he said. 'That would be an acceptable alternative theory to your guilt.'

'That is good enough for me!' Geoffrey Creach said. 'Ronnie, I am sorry, but there is no alternative but for you to accompany me to police headquarters. I will shield you from McCallum as much as I can and plead for your release, based on an alternate theory to the murder.'

'Oh, now, wait a minute!' I cried. 'Please don't tell me you are going to offer up my husband as a suspect!'

'Mrs. Watson, your husband is beyond reproach,' the solicitor said. 'I merely intend to point out to the inspector that Ronnie is no longer the only possible suspect.'

'Why can't we leave the city altogether?' Bella asked.

'How, on a train?' Mr. Creach snapped. 'Bella, the police are already checking every train in and out of the city for Ronnie. In a coach? I have to assume every cabman in town has been asked to keep a watch for him.'

'God,' Ronnie muttered. 'There is no other way, then?'

'I fear not.'

Ronnie Standish looked from Mr. Creach to me, then to John, and then he sighed heavily. 'All right, let's go.'

'Ronnie, no!' Bella shouted, rushing to him and throwing her arms around him.

'Bella,' Mr. Creach said, 'I promise you I will do whatever I can to protect him.' He managed to separate them and then led the sullen young man through the back door and into the sunlight.

'It will kill him going back into that cell,' Bella sobbed.

John took her firmly by the shoulders and gave her a small shake, just enough to reduce her hysteria. 'Listen to me,' he said, 'your becoming hysterical is of absolutely no help to your husband. Do you understand?'

'Yes,' she said, in a tiny voice.

'I shall go immediately to the nearest chemist and try to get something that will calm him while he is in gaol. It will not make his stay particularly pleasant, since incarceration is not supposed to be a holiday, but it should prevent him from becoming so agitated that he attempts to escape again.'

'You should leave here too, Bella,' I said, taking her by the arm and leading her towards the back door.

From the yard, I peeked through the door in the wall, initially to see if there was any sign of the police, and then to gauge how many pedestrians we might encounter who could possibly wonder what was taking place in the Frankham house. Finding no one in either category (except for a nurse pushing a pram, whose attention was riveted upon her squealing charge instead of the neighbourhood around her), John, Bella and I crept through and began to stroll down the street as though we belonged there. A red omnibus was stopped at the corner.

'I will meet up with you later at the hotel, Amelia, after I've secured the draught for Standish,' John said, and then dashed off to catch the bus, which was pointed towards the town.

'Where are we going?' Bella asked.

'I can't speak for you, dear, but I should like some tea and perhaps a biscuit or two, if there is an establishment near here that can accommodate us.'

'That sounds wonderful,' the girl said, appearing to fight back tears.

It turned out there was a small teahouse not far from Ashdown Crescent. Once seated at the table, we gave our orders, and then I suddenly realised that I had better make certain I was carrying enough money to pay for them. Examining the contents of my handbag, I was relieved to find a five-pound note.

I also saw something else.

'Bella, I am afraid I have a confession to make,' I said. 'I borrowed something of yours and Ronnie's. I hope you don't mind.'

'What?'

From my bag I pulled out the medallion.

'Why did you take that?' she asked, startled.

'I wanted to have it examined by an expert. I felt it might somehow be an important clue to the killing of Mr. Frankham. The artefacts Ronnie found were, after all, the cause of the argument between he and

Ronnie.'

The girl's head bowed.

Now what?

'Amelia, you may have wasted your time and effort. I believe I know why George Frankham was killed. I believe I have always known.'

'What are you saying?'

Lifting her head but refusing to look me in the eye, she went on: 'I have not been completely truthful with you, or with Mr. Creach. Those things Ronnie dug up were the cause of the argument, but not the reason it turned heated. I was the reason the quarrel became violent.'

'You?'

Her face suddenly transformed into a startling mask of anger. 'George Frankham was a beast!' she cried, then became embarrassed. More softly she elaborated: 'He would come around our house, claiming it was to meet with Ronnie, but he only came when Ronnie was out, as he well knew! While there, he ...'

'He made you indecent propositions?' I ventured.

She nodded. 'He told me he could do

things for us, if only I would do things for him. That was how the wretched man put it. He even offered me money. He was trying to turn me into a common harlot! I tried not to let him in the house, but he was stronger than I was and pushed in the door. One time ... he removed ... his clothing ... he exposed ... it made me sick ... I hated him, I hated him!'

'Oh, child,' I said, putting a comforting arm around her. 'Please forgive me, but I must ask. Did he ever succeed in his advances?'

'No!' she cried again. 'I repelled them however I could. The last time I ... I threatened him with a knife. He told me I was making a terrible mistake. He said he could ruin Ronnie, would ruin him unless I ... '

'There, child,' I said, rocking her as though she were an infant. She managed to regain control of herself as our tea and biscuits arrived.

'After the last time,' she went on, 'I told Ronnie what had been occurring. I had never seen him so angry. He swore that he would have it out with Frankham immediately. He wanted to go right then and there to Frankham's house and call him out, but I convinced him not to. The next morning, he seemed to have calmed down. He went back to work at the house, and that afternoon was when Frankham challenged him about the artefacts. That was when Ronnie threatened to kill him if he ever came around me again.'

'Dear Lord,' I moaned. 'Why haven't you told this to anyone?'

'I was afraid it would make the case against Ronnie even worse. An argument over a bunch of artefacts was hardly like a reason to kill someone. Even a jury could be made to see that. But protecting your own wife against … against … '

She collapsed into sobs again, and I felt miserable. The situation against Ronnie had just worsened tenfold with this bit of information. No other theory — not the unfounded, but suspected, idea that someone was planting evidence that deliberately pointed towards him; not the bizarre possibility that George Frankham was a member of some strange group of pagans, and that had somehow led to his death, as well as that of the photographer, Mr.

Allardice; not even the ridiculous smoke-and-mirrors argument that John had done it — held the potential weight in a courtroom that the disclosure that Ronnie Standish had threatened a man who was attempting to seduce his wife would carry with it. What could be done now?

'Bella,' I sighed, 'I fear I have failed you. You asked for help and I have been able to offer none. I should never have come here.'

'I am still glad you did. No one except Mr. Creach even bothered to consider Ronnie's innocence. You at least believed it.'

'I believed it because you believed it, Bella.' A terrible thought then hit me. 'You *do* genuinely believe that Ronnie is innocent, don't you? You have not been misleading me about that as well?'

'I *believed* Ronnie was innocent, I truly did, but now ... '

'But now what, Bella?'

'I don't know,' she moaned. 'The last two days have revealed a side of him that I have not seen before, an angrier, harsher side. He has acted as though he is hiding something. And now that horrible business of the button ... Amelia, what am I to do if

Ronnie is … is … '

'Guilty of murder? I do not know, Bella, I really do not know. But if there is anything else, anything at all, that you have not told me, whether you believe it hurts Ronnie's case or helps it, you must do so.'

She shook her head. 'No, there is nothing else.'

I wished I could believe her.

I also wished that I could have banished from my mind the terrible realization that had just struck me.

Having finished our tea, we walked back in silence and without incident back to her neighbourhood. When we were a block away, Bella asked: 'Aren't we going in through the back?'

'No, dear, we cannot do that,' I told her. 'There might be a policeman stationed there. We will have to go in through the front, and you must still pretend to be Missy, since you are still supposed to be in the house. You are, after all, still wearing her clothing. Once inside, you can trade clothes and she and I will leave together.'

At the entrance to Albert Street, I stopped and peered around the corner to see who, if anyone, remained stationed out on her doorstep. I saw PC Richter at his post, as though he was growing there rooted, but alone. 'All we have to do is get past the constable,' I said. 'Keep your head down and try not to face him.'

'Very well.'

With Bella at my side, I leisurely walked up Albert Street until I had come to the house.

'How d'you do, ma'am?' PC Richter asked, brightly. 'Been a while since you was here.'

'Yes, I wanted Bella to get some much-needed rest.'

'Haven't seen or heard hide nor hair of her since the day that man was snooping 'round the backyard.'

'A man was snooping around the backyard?' I asked, then remembered the subterfuge I had enacted on the constable. 'Oh, yes, of course. Did you ever find out who it was?'

'Probably one of them press hounds,' he said. 'He ain't been back.'

'Good. Is Miss Cornwell here?'

'The lawyer's girl? No ma'am, haven't

seen her today.'

'May we go in?'

'Certainly, ma'am.'

Things were going swimmingly until Bella absentmindedly said: 'Oh no, I don't have a key.'

'What's that, miss?' PC Richter said.

I quickly stood in front of her and said, 'Oh, she said she didn't have tea.' Taking the girl by the arm, I approached the door and began knocking. 'Bella? It's Amelia and Missy. Please open the door.' All the while I was praying that Missy would get the message and remember that she was still supposed to be Bella, before everything fell apart.

Fortune was with us as Missy unlocked the door and creaked it open, never making herself seen. The real Bella and I quickly dashed inside. 'Oh, I am glad this is over with,' she said.

'Mum, does that mean I can leave now?' Missy asked, pleadingly.

'Yes, dear, we will both leave together,' I said. 'The reporters have gone and Bella should be able to come and go freely now.'

'Thank god for that,' Bella sighed. 'Oh, I

must clean up and get out of these clothes. You were lucky, Missy. You could put on another dress of mine whenever you wanted.'

'Yes'm,' Missy acknowledged, grimly, 'but now I have to put those clothes you've been wearing back on.'

'Only long enough to get out of here, Missy,' I said. 'You can change when we get back to the hotel.'

Both girls repaired upstairs to change, returning some minutes later in their proper clothing, though Missy appeared distressed. 'There's a tear in it!' she complained, holding the top part of her skirt. 'My best dress!'

'I will get you a new one,' I said, 'but for now, we must be on our way. Bella, you should see us off at the door, for the sake of the constable.' She did so, quite convincingly, taking special care to speak with PC Richter and thanking Missy profusely for staying and helping her with the housework. In fact, she was on the verge of overplaying it and giving the game away when I finally cut her off and Missy and I took our leave.

Missy complained about her dress all the way to the Roman Hotel, so I was quite happy to deposit her in the room Bella had been using in order to freshen up and change, and retire to my own room, where I found John busily jotting down notes of some sort on a sheet of paper.

'Hello, darling,' I said. 'How is Ronnie?'

'As well as can be expected,' he said. 'He is back in a cell, unfortunately, despite that lawyer's best argument, but I was indeed able to procure a calming draught for him. Have you learned anything new?'

'I don't know,' I sighed. 'I feel like I must sit down and force myself to think this entire thing through.'

'Perhaps you should take up the pipe.'

'That is all I need on top of everything else.'

'Amelia, perhaps it is time to at least consider the possibility that Standish is guilty,' John was saying. 'I know you do not wish him to be, but the evidence is simply too strong to keep resisting.'

I sighed again. 'It is become even worse than that, darling. I am now looking at it from the standpoint of not wanting *Bella* to be the murderer.' I explained to him the real reason for Ronnie's threat to George Frankham, and the uncomfortable fact that only Bella had easy access to the items that served as the strongest evidence against her husband.

John set down his pen. 'Great Scott, you don't suppose that button was pulled off of Frankham's coat while he was making an advance upon Bella, do you?'

'I don't know,' I said, 'though I must confess that the business of that button has bothered me from the start. Something about it is not right. Let's say someone is attacking you with a club or a bludgeon, and it was impossible for you to flee, as appears to have been the case with Mr. Allardice. What would you do?'

'Try to protect myself, I suppose. Try to block the blows, or repel the attacker.'

'Exactly,' I said. 'You would try to push the man away from you, most likely using either open hands or clenched fists. But pulling off a button implies that you are *grasping* at the other person and attempting to pull them *towards* you, and coming away only with the button.'

'Perhaps the button came off accidentally.'

'That still would not explain why it was

closed so tightly in the man's fist,' I argued. 'If someone were attacking me, and during the struggle I somehow ended up with a button from his coat, I would put my hands up to protect myself, and in the process drop the button.'

John rose from the desk and started pacing back and forth. 'What about this, then? You try to push your assailant away, to no avail. He strikes you upon the head and you lose your balance and slump against him. You start to fall, but on the way down, your hand rakes the front of his coat, pulling off the button. You fall to the floor, unconscious, with the button still in your hand.' He stopped pacing and regarded me soberly. 'Not very convincing, is it?'

'No,' I said, seating myself on the edge of the bed, 'and that is what has been bothering me. In all your cases with Mr. Holmes, John, how many have involved a tell-tale clue such as that?'

'None, that I recall.'

'Because such a clue is too pat, too convenient, too fictional. I have encountered it several times, however, in the pages of a book or on stage.'

'What are you saying? That someone deliberately planted that button in the man's hand?'

'Precisely. The killer knew it would be discovered by someone and that it would ultimately point to Ronnie.'

'If that is true, we have a devious killer.'

'Or one conversant with inferior literature.'

'Good heavens, dear, don't tell me you now suspect our Missy.'

I laughed — for the first time in days, it seemed like. 'No, darling, it is bad enough to suspect Bella.'

'Well, I have only seen the girl briefly, but it was enough to prevent me from casting her in the role of Lady Macbeth.'

In my heart of hearts, I knew he was right. Bella was no more a killer than I was. It was all so infuriatingly puzzling.

A knock then came at the door, which I opened to find Mrs. Grimes.

'That lawyer, Mr. Crutch, is downstairs calling on you,' she said.

'Mr. Creach, you mean?'

'Himself.'

'Very well, I shall be down presently.'

'Yes, we'll both be down,' John said.

The bar of the Roman Hotel consisted of a fold-down counter that was just large enough to hold a row of glasses. There we found Geoffrey Creach, draining the last of a bottle of ale. 'Join me?' he asked in a dejected tone of voice.

'I'll have a whisky,' John said, agreeably.

'Nothing for me,' I told the landlady. Turning to Mr. Creach, I said, 'Surely you did not ask us down here simply to have drinking companions.'

'No, Mrs. Watson,' he said, ordering another bottle of Worthington's ale from the landlady. 'I received a telegram from the London offices of the esteemed Horace Filcher, esquire, rejecting Ronnie's case. That is the seventh barrister who has turned us down.'

'I have never heard of a case so hopeless that no one would even take it up,' John said.

'Neither have I, prior to this.'

'There must be someone, somewhere, who is willing to take it on,' I said.

'Oh, there no doubt is, but it would not be someone of the calibre that I was hoping to attract. What Ronnie needs is a top legal mind, not a second-rate Temple Bar bumbler. I am at my wits' end. Worse, far worse, I must ask myself how much longer I can rely on my initial belief that Ronnie Standish is innocent.'

''Twas guilty he was from the start, he was,' Mrs. Grimes chimed in. 'Sure, and the papers said as much.'

'Not everything that appears in the papers is the truth, Mrs. Grimes,' I said. To Mr. Creach, I added: 'Have you confessed your waning confidence to Ronnie and Bella?'

'No. I tried to talk to Ronnie at the gaol today, but was unable to hold a conversation. He appeared dazed.'

'The effects of that draught I gave him,' John said. 'I hope the police are not overdosing him.'

The once-confident, even brash, solicitor held his head in his hands and moaned, 'I wish I knew what to do for him.'

John set down his glass. 'I know what I can do. I am not unknown amongst legal circles in London. I can go up there and speak to a few acquaintances at the Bailey, try to convince them that the case is worth taking on. I could leave on the first morning train.'

'Really, Dr. Watson, there is no need for your getting involved.'

'I am involved already.'

'And, coming from the great city, you will of course succeed where I have failed, is that it?' the solicitor asked, betraying a peevish tone.

'Honestly, I do not know,' John replied. 'Perhaps I will be no more successful than you have been. But isn't the fate of poor Standish at least worth making the effort?'

'Of course it is,' I said, and I must admit I was a bit annoyed at the pouty way Mr. Creach was accepting John's offer of help. Then again, the man was probably exhausted, as well as a bit tipsy.

'It is settled, then. The station is not far; I shall walk down there and find out the timetable for tomorrow's trains, and plan to leave as early as possible tomorrow morning.' Finishing his whisky, he went straight outside.

Once he was gone, I said: 'If you don't mind my saying so, Mr. Creach, you were not exactly gracious in accepting John's help.'

'I did not ask for John's help,' he replied.

'Even if it is Ronnie's last chance?'

The solicitor drained his ale and set the bottle down with a slam. 'Ever defensive of your spouse, aren't you? Most, I suppose, would call that a noble attribute. Just remember this: it was through defending his spouse that Ronnie got into trouble in the first place. Good night, Mrs. Watson.' He turned and lurched towards the front door.

'Mr. Creach, you forgot your stick,' I said, motioning to the umbrella holder that he had walked past.

'What? Oh, right. Thank you.' Taking up his stick and his hat, he left.

Mrs. Grimes watched him go, before wiping up the bar. 'Back in my country we have a word for rude menfolk like that, but 'tis not repeatin' it I'll be.'

'We have a word for them here, too, Mrs. Grimes. Lawyers. I shall be going back upstairs.'

Experiencing a rare moment of quiet in the room, I attempted to read, but found that I could not get my mind off of the case enough to concentrate on the pages. I was still attempting to make sense of what was happening around me an hour later, when John returned.

'Seeing as how the police station is so close to the train station, I stopped in at the gaol to see how Standish was faring,' he said, taking off his jacket.

'And?'

'I believe Creach was exaggerating when he said he was dazed. He appeared quite lucid as I explained to him my mission to London, and told him that everything would turn out for the better. I am confident that he will not attempt to escape again. Even if he wanted to, there is no way he would make it out of the cell. They have doubled the guard on him.'

'Will things really turn out for the better, darling?'

John sighed as he sat on the edge of the bed. 'I cannot see how. The evidence against the lad appears so overwhelming that I have to ask myself whether Creach has not in fact deliberately avoided trying to engage a barrister, despite his claims of having been refused, just so this case will not come to trial any time soon. Once that evidence is set before a jury, I would not give tuppence for Standish's chances. His only hope is that the real killer — if, indeed, it is not he — is discovered.'

'Which is exactly what I hoped I would be able to do,' I sighed. 'Oh, John, I have failed miserably. I feel so helpless.'

'There, there, I shall do everything I can,' he said, rising. 'My train leaves shortly before seven tomorrow morning, so I need to get some sleep.'

Neither John nor I spoke as we prepared for bed. Once he had doused the lights and climbed in beside me, immediately I relaxed. Within minutes his breathing became slow and measured, and I felt that odd, indescribable sensation of ease that came from knowing he was there, but asleep. I could feel myself starting to drift off, being held awake only by ...

By what?

By some disconnected thought that would not let my mind fully relax enough to fall to sleep. It is, alas, a sensation I feel often when some niggling little idea runs around in my brain, never quite stepping into clarity or focus, but just active enough to keep the rest of my mind searching for it. It was a thought that desperately wanted to announce its presence, but did not know how to begin. After spinning about for what seemed like an hour, however, the thought went away. Perhaps it was exhausted as well.

I fell into a dreamless sleep after that, and remembered nothing until the sensation of my elbow being squeezed, gently but firmly, which was John's way of awakening me. Opening my eyes, I saw that he was already dressed. 'What time is it?' I moaned.

'A bit after six in the morning,' he said. 'I have to leave now in order to make the train. I shall be back as soon as I am able.'

'Good luck darling.'

He left quietly, and I went back to sleep for an undetermined amount of time, only to abruptly awaken again by lurching upright in the bed. My hand flew to my forehead as that annoying little thought that had been tormenting me last evening suddenly announced itself with the force of a brass overture.

'Good heavens, how could I have been so blind?' I said aloud.

Suddenly I had a very good idea of who had killed George Frankham.

9

Suspicion of the killer's identity was of little use if there was no way to support it with proof, and the evidence was tenuous at best. It was not half as strong as the circumstantial evidence that had been used to condemn Ronnie. And yet it all made sense. It was, in fact, the only solution that did.

Before I did anything else, I had to speak with Bella. As soon as I was dressed, I dashed out of the hotel, skipping breakfast, in order to make my way to Albert Street. I had walked the distance between the Roman Hotel and the Standish house so frequently that I could now do it without even thinking.

PC Richter was stationed in front — naturally — looking very tired, as though he had been standing vigil all night. 'Good morning, Constable,' I said. 'Is Bella in?'

'Morning, ma'am,' he said with a yawn. 'I've not seen her come out.'

I rapped on the door and Bella answered

it, looking somewhat more fit and rested than PC Richter. 'Amelia, is there any news of Ronnie?' she asked immediately.

I quickly entered the house and shut the door behind me. 'I'm afraid not. John is on his way to London to try and engage a barrister.'

'But I thought Mr. Creach was doing that.'

'Yes, dear, but … Bella, we need to talk.' I manoeuvred her to the sitting room, which was still curtained and dark, and sat her down on the sofa. 'What I am about to ask you is very, very important. The advance that Mr. Frankham made on you — '

'Oh, please, I don't wish to talk about that,' she whined.

'Bella, you must, if we are to have any hope of helping Ronnie. You told me that you had informed Ronnie of Mr. Frankham's actions and that was what prompted the fight between the two of them.'

'Yes,' she said in a very small voice.

'You also said that you had told absolutely no one else, save for me. Is that right?'

'Yes, you and Ronnie are the only ones who know.'

'Could Ronnie have told someone?'

'Who would he tell?'

'Well, Mr. Creach, perhaps?'

Bella shook her head. 'Ronnie would not tell Mr. Creach.'

'How can you be so certain?'

'Because I know he would not. Why is this so important?'

'Child, you are evading the question,' I said in my best headmistress voice. 'Please answer me.' The artifice appeared to be working: immediately Bella straightened up and took on the demeanour of a slightly frightened schoolgirl. 'How do you know that Ronnie would not tell Mr. Creach? After all, it is a justifiable explanation for his becoming angry with the man.'

'Yes, and it is also a justifiable explanation for his killing him!' Bella cried. 'And if anyone else were to learn of it, things would be just that much worse for Ronnie. That is why I ... I — '

'You what, Bella?'

'I threatened to leave Ronnie if he ever told.' She collapsed into sobs.

'Oh, dear God,' I muttered, sitting back down on the couch. 'That poor boy doesn't have enough to worry about without the fear that his wife is going to run away if he tells the truth in his own defence?'

'I wish I could apologise to him,' she sobbed. 'I know it was a harsh thing to do, but I was trying to prevent him from saying something that could make the situation even worse for him. You do understand, don't you, Miss Pettigrew?'

Now it was back to *Miss Pettigrew.* My little charade had worked too well. I put an arm around the girl.

We were interrupted just then by an insistent knock on the front door. I went to it and called out for the identity of the caller before opening.

'Is that you, Mrs. Watson?' a woman's voice called back. 'It is Kitty Cornwell.'

'Kitty,' I shouted back, 'are you alone?'

'Yes. Please open the door.'

The sudden appearance of Geoffrey Creach's betrothed was certain to complicate things, but there seemed to be little I could do in the way of preventing her. I cracked open the door enough to see Kitty standing there, with PC Richter behind her. 'I told her you were inside, ma'am,' he said, almost apologetically.

'I must speak with you, Mrs. Watson,' Kitty pleaded. 'I tried your rooming house, but you had already left. I thought you might be here.'

'Come in, Kitty,' I said, opening the door enough to let her rush in.

'Miss Cornwell,' Bella said upon seeing her. 'Amelia, this is Mr. Creach's fiancée.'

'Yes, I know, we've met. Why are you here, Kitty?'

'I have information from Geoffrey regarding the case. He has had photographs made from those plates.'

'The ones of George Frankham?'

'No, it isn't Frankham, Mrs. Watson. It is another man altogether. Geoffrey believes it to be an image of the murderer himself!'

Bella gasped. 'Who is it?' she cried, rushing towards Kitty. 'Please, tell me! Tell me and then come to the gaol with me so that we can put the evidence before the police and get Ronnie released!'

'We cannot go to the police,' Kitty said, grimly. 'The man in the photographs is the police inspector who is heading up the case.'

'Inspector McCallum?' I said in disbelief.

'That is what Geoffrey says. His theory is that the inspector is trying to convict Mr. Standish in order to obscure his own guilt.'

Bella's eyes grew frantically wide. 'Amelia, what are we going to do?'

Indeed, what was I going to do? The game was becoming serious now, unbeknownst to Bella — or to Kitty, for that matter — and the slightest misstep on my part might result in disaster.

'Geoffrey feels that we are all in danger,' Kitty went on. 'He thinks the inspector is beginning to realise that we suspect him.'

'Good gracious, Kitty, I question whether Inspector McCallum has the intellectual capacity to begin to realise when he is standing in the rain.'

'He has fooled us all with that boor act, but he can no longer fool Geoffrey. He thought it was best, Mrs. Watson, if you were to leave immediately and go back to London. He has taken the photographs and is on his way to the regional police offices in Bristol. Before going, he asked me to come and urge you to leave.'

'You're not going to go, are you?' Bella

cried. 'Please, Miss Pettigrew, you can't!'

I turned to look at her: so young, so vulnerable. Then I turned back to Kitty Cornwell, who asked, 'Miss Pettigrew?'

'My name when I first met Bella, but that is not important. Kitty, have you actually seen these photographs yourself?'

'No, I am only telling you what Geoffrey told me.'

'I see.' I studied her strong, worried face for a moment, and then said: 'Thank you, Kitty, for passing along the information to me, but I am afraid that I must stay here, at least until my husband John returns from London.'

'Did you not hear what I said?'

'Every word.' I turned once more to Bella, took her by the shoulders, and again adopted the manner of her former governess. 'I will not leave you, Bella, but there is something I must ask you to do. You must stay here and open the door to no one except me. Is that clear?'

'Yes.'

'Do you have enough food for another day?'

'I think so.'

'Good. I will speak to Constable Richter on my way out and request that he likewise allow no one inside except me. Now, I believe I will go back to my hotel. Kitty, would you mind coming with me?'

'Well, I suppose not.'

'Excellent. Goodbye, Bella, I shall be in touch soon.'

I marched to the front door, with Kitty Cornwell in step behind me, and exited onto the porch. As I had promised Bella, I had a word with PC Richter, who nodded in agreement, even though he looked a bit puzzled. 'I cannot explain it all now, but I will,' I told him. Then I walked down to the street, massaging my temples as I went, and praying that I really knew what I was doing.

'You look troubled, Mrs. Watson,' Kitty said.

Troubled seemed to be an excellent way of describing the search for some means of telling a woman to her face that her fiancé was a double murderer ... for I was now completely convinced that Geoffrey Creach was the killer of George Frankham and the photographer J. Allardice!

Why the man had killed them was

something I was not able to divine, but with the assumption of his guilt, every other element of the case fell into place. Creach had killed George Frankham, and then used the incident of the argument between Frankham and Ronnie to implicate the latter. Then he had promptly volunteered his services as solicitor — not to aid Ronnie, as he proclaimed, but to secretly do everything possible to ensure his conviction! I now realised that the solicitor had avoided seeking out a barrister under the pretence of not being able to engage one, not to postpone Ronnie from going to trial, but rather to make certain that no competent counsel would take the case and, in the process, discover the truth about the killings and exonerate Ronnie.

He had known Ronnie to be hiding in Frankham's house. He had visited him there before the murder of Mr. Allardice, and had probably seen that Ronnie was wearing Frankham's clothing. He could have obtained that button from Frankham's jacket to place in Mr. Allardice's hand as a clue. He had removed the photographic plates from the police station, and I did not for a moment believe that it was Inspector McCallum's image on those photographs, but Geoffrey Creach's. If they *had* shown the inspector, he surely would have kept the plates himself.

Poor Kitty had simply passed along the lies that had been fed to her by her beloved in order to deceive me.

We shared not a word between us the entire distance back to the Roman Hotel, and once there I led her straight to my room, closing the door behind us. Taking a deep breath, I said: 'Kitty, Geoffrey is the killer, not Inspector McCallum.'

For a second she looked stunned, but it was chased away a second later by a surprising explosion of laughter. 'That is the most outlandish thing I have ever heard!' she cried.

'Please, listen to me. I believe he also killed the photographer, though I don't have the slightest clue as to why.'

'But this is absurd! How could you come to such a ridiculous conclusion?'

'It is only ridiculous if you are close to the suspect,' I said. 'Geoffrey himself handed me a problem that I could not solve. You see, the argument that took place between Ronnie Standish and George Frankham has been characterised as having been about Ronnie's taking liberties in digging on Frankham's property.'

'That is common knowledge.'

'Exactly. But Bella Standish confided in me that the argument was really about Frankham having made overtures towards her. That is what incensed Ronnie.'

Kitty's expression turned thoughtful. 'Really? I had no idea.'

'But Bella swore to me that she had told no one of the real reason for the argument, and she also threatened to leave Ronnie if he breathed a word of it to anyone.'

'So?'

'So, how did Geoffrey know about it?'

'I'm sure he didn't.'

'Oh, but he did. He said as much to me last night at the bar of this hotel. I believe his exact words were, 'it was through defending his spouse that Ronnie got into trouble in the first place', and I knew immediately what he meant. But it dawned on me later that *he* should not have known that.'

'Perhaps one of the witnesses to the argument told him.'

'The witnesses were all interviewed by the members of the press,' I countered. 'Had any one of them mentioned Bella as a motive, I assure you it would have made its way into the papers. No, there is only one way he could have learned that bit of information. Geoffrey was present during the fight between Ronnie and Frankham.'

'What?'

'He had to be there, somewhere — hidden in the shadows, perhaps, but close enough to hear the accusations and threats being thrown back and forth.'

'You are talking nonsense!' Kitty cried. 'I won't listen!'

'You must listen! The presumption that Geoffrey Creach was in that house answers so many questions. It was Geoffrey who realised that he could kill Frankham, and then plant the evidence so it pointed straight towards Ronnie. It was Geoffrey who picked up Ronnie's measuring tool at Frankham's house and left it at the scene of the crime. It was Geoffrey who took the photograph from Frankham's house and then tried to destroy its frame. It was Geoffrey who placed the button from Frankham's coat into the hands of Mr. Allardice, knowing that Ronnie would be suspected. He has been secretly orchestrating every step of this investigation, and I have no doubt would continue orchestrating the trial, to ensure that Ronnie Standish will go to the gallows for his crimes.'

Kitty Cornwell turned away and buried her head in her hands. 'Why would Geoffrey do such terrible things as you describe?'

'All of the terrible things, as you say, have emanated from the killing of George Frankham. As to why that murder was committed, I really don't know. Perhaps you could shed light on it.'

She glared at me with alarm. 'Me?'

'You know Geoffrey better than anyone. Is there any reason you can think of that he would wish to dispose of Mr. Frankham?'

'He didn't even know the man!' She leapt up and started for the door, leaving a trail of heated anger behind her. 'Mrs. Watson, I came to you in friendship, and all you have done is turned this back on Geoffrey and accuse him of reprehensible things! I will

247

hear no more!' The force with which she tore open the door and stormed out was rather unbecoming in a woman.

'Please be careful, Kitty,' I called to her back, but within seconds she was gone from the house.

Mrs. Grimes appeared at the foot of the stairs a second later and said, ''Tis strong emotions you stir in people, I'll give you that.'

'Everyone should have a special talent, Mrs. Grimes,' I sighed. 'That appears to be mine.'

'Can I get you anything?'

'No, thank you.' I could feel a serious headache coming on, so I went back inside the room while I contemplated what to do next. What I should do was go straight to the police station and tell my theory to Inspector McCallum — but how much good would that do? The man seemed incapable of logic. Flashes of pain were now pounding through my head in defiance of any cogent thought. Maybe if I just lay down for a moment, the red veil of pain would lift and my thoughts would clear. I went to the basin, took up a cloth and wetted it, then made my way to the bed and stretched out with the damp cloth on my forehead. Yes, that was better … much better.

The next thing I heard was a strange tapping noise, and after a moment's disorientation, I realised it was someone at the door of my room. 'Come in,' I called out, wearily, but no one did. Rising, I went to the door, and realised I had locked it from inside.

'You locked me out, mum,' Missy said, looking hurt.

'Oh, I am sorry, child. I didn't mean to. What have you there?'

She handed me an envelope. 'A note came for you.'

'A note? What time is it?'

'Half-past seven o'clock, mum.'

'Oh, good heavens,' I moaned. 'I've slept most of the day.'

'Don't I know it,' the girl replied. 'I've been doing housework for Mrs. Grimes, hoping at some point you'd open the door. I don't mind the dusting and sweeping, but 'tis gardening I don't like.'

Good heavens, the girl was even beginning to talk like the Irishwoman!

'Forgive me, Missy, really. Come in.'

After splashing a bit of water onto my face from the basin, I towelled off and examined the note, which read:

Mrs. Watson:

You were right! Geoffrey is a villain! Now I am in grave danger.

Must talk with you urgently. Meet me at the train station at nine this evening. Please tell no one. I do not want word somehow getting back to Geoffrey.

Had she been so stupid as to confront her fiancé directly? Kitty did not strike me as a foolish person, so she must have discovered some evidence which she was willing to confide in me. But nine o'clock was nearly two hours away, and I loathed waiting.

Mrs. Grimes was making a fine game stew, judging from its aroma; I tried to eat some of it when it arrived, but my focus was more on the clock in the dining room. Finally, at a little before nine, I set out.

'Do you need me to come with you,

mum?' Missy asked.

'No, dear, you stay here; but do no more housework. You have the night off.'

I had brought only a light jacket with me to Bath, which was barely sufficient against the country chill as I left for the train station. I walked briskly and kept my wits about me, turning to investigate any noise I heard on any side. I cannot say what I might have been expecting to happen, but whatever it was, I hoped I was ready for it.

The train station appeared to be deserted. I looked around for any sign of Kitty Cornwell, and found none. I heard the abbey bell chime nine o'clock. Now I was becoming worried. What if Mr. Creach had found out about Kitty's plans and had prevented her?

It was then I heard the sound of a coach approaching. A hansom was speeding up behind the platform, and a figure leaned out of the window. 'Mrs. Watson!' a voice cried.

'Kitty?' I called back.

'Yes, hurry, get in!'

The cab pulled up directly in front of me and stopped just long enough for me to dash inside, and then it was off again.

'Kitty, what is all this?'

'Geoffrey found out that I was coming here,' she said, breathlessly. 'I just managed to escape.'

'We must go to the police.'

'No! We cannot do that! You see, Geoffrey was not lying about the inspector's involvement in the murders. They did it together!'

'Mr. Creach and Inspector McCallum? What on earth for?'

'It has something to do with pagan religious ceremonies. That's all I know.'

So that was it. Both Creach and McCallum were members of the mysterious cult of Cam, along with Frankham. Their constant sparring must be nothing more than a bizarre Punch-and-Judy show staged for the benefit of onlookers, including me, and that would explain why the inspector had treated the evidence John and I had found in the photographer's back room so cavalierly; he knew his accomplice would take care of it.

The cab bounced indelicately over the streets. In the dark, I could not see where we were headed. 'Why don't we go back to my hotel?' I asked. 'We will both be safe there.'

'No, there is a better place,' Kitty replied. 'Where?'

She did not answer, but after a few minutes I could hear the faint rush of water. We were somewhere near the river.

'Kitty, please tell me where we are going.'

'I cannot take the chance of telling you.'

'Kitty, I do not understand.' Just then, the cab bounced and tipped suddenly to the right so severely that for a moment I was afraid it was going to turn over. I lunged towards the other side, hoping my weight may help keep it on balance. I knocked on the roof and cried, 'Driver! Be careful, will you?'

'Sorry ma'am,' he called back; but just for a moment, I thought I heard him laugh.

'You look frightened, Mrs. Watson?' Kitty said.

'I confess that I am becoming so.'

'Why?'

'Why? Because I am in a speeding, inexpertly-driven coach, heading off to heaven knows where, for some unknown reason. You asked me to meet you at the train station, which I did, but now I fear I am being abducted. But even more ominous than that, Kitty, is the fact that you no longer seem to be afraid.'

'Why should I be? Things are going exactly as planned.' She drew her hand out from under the folds in her dress and pointed a small pistol at me. 'Please don't try to do anything foolish,' she said, her smile widening in a show of enjoyment at my discomfort. 'We will arrive at our destination soon.' Then, much more loudly, she called out: 'We will be there soon, won't we, darling?'

The ceiling window of the hansom slid open. For the first time I saw the face of the driver, and I gasped.

'There in two shakes,' said Geoffrey Creach, who then slid the window shut again.

10

Dropping all pretence of conviviality, Kitty Cornwell said, 'So, you London bitch, there is nothing for you to do but sit quietly and wait.'

'Sitting quietly and waiting is not my strong suit,' I said, desperately striving for an insouciant tone to mask the fact that I was shaking all over.

She pointed the pistol straight at my heart. 'And I should warn you that I am an excellent shot.'

'I suppose Geoffrey finds that admirable in a woman.'

Kitty chuckled darkly. 'There is very little Geoffrey finds admirable in a woman.'

We carried on in silence and darkness for several more minutes, and then the ride became even rougher, as if we had left the road altogether and were travelling over grass and rock. Through the window of the cab I could see that we were entering a wooded area. I could also hear the sound of rushing water, and knew we were near the river. The cab jerked to a stop and Geoffrey Creach jumped down from the driver's seat. Then, opening the door, he pulled me out, while Kitty followed with the pistol.

'Let me go!' I shouted, attempting to fight back, but Creach's hold was too tight. Suddenly a sound cut through the night, a pained kind of moaning coming from the river's edge. I stopped struggling and looked towards the noise. In the dim illumination of the cab's headlights, I could make out a shape on the ground. It was a person, a man, who was apparently trussed up with rope. The figure moaned again and sluggishly raised its head, and when it did so my heart sank and I screamed, 'Dear God!'

It was my husband!

'John!' I cried, breaking out of Creach's grip and rushing to my husband. I knelt down, and while I did not have the strength to pull him to his feet, I gently picked up his head and placed it on my lap, cradling it. 'Darling, are you hurt? What have they done to you?' I could not find any injury, but he was acting as though he were only now regaining consciousness; his head lolled about and he seemed unable to form words. 'What is wrong with him?' I shouted back to the murderous couple.

'I have given him a dose of his own medicine,' Creach said, 'that draught he secured for Standish. Your husband is surprisingly strong for a man of his age. It took several doses to put him out. By contrast, it only took one for the owner of this cab.'

'Why is he here? He is supposed to be in London.'

'Yes, well, I met him at the station this morning with an urgent request, and ensured that he never made it onto the train — as I would have done for you too, had you followed my instructions and fled the city. I could not run the risk of having him succeed in attracting an outside barrister to the case who might stumble upon some questions that I cannot afford to have answered.'

'What are you going to do with us?'

'Well, you are going to die, of course,' he said. 'I wish there were some way I could have got Standish out of jail so I could have staged your deaths to implicate him, but one plays the hand one is dealt. So now your deaths must look accidental. Fortunately, the doctor's reputation as an amateur investigator could very easily lead to such an assumption. You see, at the water's edge is a boat, a rather decrepit and leaky one. A native of the city would certainly know better than to try and take such a boat onto the Avon in the dead of night. But outsiders, unfamiliar with the current of the river, might attempt such an act and, alas, drown.'

'You will not succeed in this,' I said, hoping that I sounded defiant, when, in fact, I was all but convinced that Geoffrey Creach would succeed in killing us and deflecting the blame. Why, why, *why* had I ever come to Bath?

'Oh, I think I will,' the solicitor replied. 'I have succeeded thus far, after all.'

I turned to his fiancée, hoping to ignite some small spark of humanity in her. 'Kitty, please,' I said, 'I understand your wanting to protect the man you love, but can I not appeal to you as a woman to stop this madness?'

'Appeal to me as a woman?' Kitty replied, and then began to laugh. Reaching up, she grabbed the pompadour of her hair, and pulled. Her hair came off in her hand, revealing a close-cropped, nearly-shaven head underneath. 'Surprised?' Kitty said in a huskier version of her voice.

'Good heavens … you … are … a … '

'A man,' Kitty Cornwell said, keeping the gun trained on me. 'I was born Christopher. My family called me Kit as a boy. Kitty came later. We must keep up appearances, you see, for Geoffrey's sake. He would be ostracised from his profession if anyone knew about us. While I happen to believe that he possesses the intellect of Oscar Wilde, I have no desire to see him share his fate — banished, broken, hated, languishing in prison, all because he has indulged in the love that dare not speak its name in our ignorant society. It is necessary for Geoffrey to be seen with a woman; therefore, he shall be seen with a woman.'

'May I guess why George Frankham was killed?' I asked, hoping to forestall the inevitable for a little longer. 'It had nothing to do with that medallion or any other artefact Ronnie found; instead, it was because he discovered the truth about you.'

'Nothing of the sort,' Geoffrey Creach replied. 'He had to die because he was standing in my way. You already know about the worship of Cam, and you already know that Frankham and that fool Allardice were part of it. What you may not know is that Frankham was the cult's leader, its priest. It was to him that one had to appeal to be considered for membership. I learned that from a local justice who was a member but was no longer interested in attending the ceremonies. I intended to fill that opening, but Frankham, damn his soul, refused. I was not a true believer, he said. I was not devout enough for his precious little Hellfire Club. And it was true, I cared nothing for his ridiculous water god.'

'Why were you so desperate to become a member, then?' I asked.

'Because the group, under Frankham, had transformed into an alliance of the most powerful and influential men in this city. Being in that kind of gathering could mean everything for me professionally. And it will. My membership is being taken up by the new priest.'

'The new priest?'

'Yes, it appears my friend the justice has returned to the fold to take over for Frankham.'

'Why did Allardice have to die?'

'Allardice suspected that I was responsible for Frankham's death. He knew about my attempts to join the group, and he knew that I had been rebuffed. On a hunch, he sent a letter to me outlining his suspicions and demanding a certain amount of money in return for his not going to the police.'

'You killed him to prevent him from blackmailing you.'

'You are not understanding it, Mrs. Watson,' Mr. Creach said. 'I did not kill anyone.'

'Then who?' As soon as the words were out of my mouth, I knew the answer. 'You, Kitty, you killed them both?'

'It was too dangerous for Geoffrey to do the killings himself,' Kitty said. 'What if he were seen and recognised by someone? So I went in his place. Dressed in men's clothing, I am unrecognizable to anyone in the city. Even if someone had seen me and had been able to offer the police a description, that man would never be found.

261

I followed Frankham that night, ready to attack whenever the proper moment arose. When I saw him cut through the abbey grounds near the Great Bath, I knew that the chance had come. Hidden by the darkness, I moved ahead of him, climbed up onto the terrace, and lured him up there. After I had clubbed him, I dropped that wooden ruler that Geoffrey had taken from the excavation site in order to lead the police to Standish's doorstep. As for Allardice, I went there as a customer. After dispatching him to his reward, I put that button in his hand and then searched the place for any evidence he had against Geoffrey, but could not find any.'

'You have no idea how relieved I was, Mrs. Watson, to learn that you and the good doctor had turned up the sort of evidence we were looking for in Allardice's studio,' Mr. Creach said.

'Those plates, you mean?'

'Exactly. One was indeed of Frankham, dressed in his priest's robes, but the second was the truly dangerous one: it was a photographic copy of the letter that Allardice had sent to me. Had that idiot McCallum actually examined it, I would be a dead egg by now. But we have nothing to worry about from him. He has taken the bait exactly as I have fed it to him, and nothing will sway his mind away from Standish's guilt.'

'So, under the presumption of helping him, you are going to forfeit the life of a man who has done nothing to you?'

'I am someone who knows what he wants and goes after it,' Mr. Creach said. 'And if a gift happens to come along in the process, I am certainly not going to refuse it. Standish was such a gift. That button was a gift as well. Do you know where I found it? It was at the bottom of the bag that Frankham had left on the street when he climbed the wall onto the terrace of the Bath, which Kitty took with her after dispatching him. That was the bag in which he carried his robe to the ceremony, and then stashed his street clothes in while it was going on. It must have fallen off of his coat at some point as he stuffed it in or pulled it out, and he never found it. I thought little of it, either, until I saw Standish wearing Frankham's clothing. I could hardly believe the serendipity.'

'Geoffrey, we are wasting time,' Kitty said. 'She does not need to know everything.'

'Oh, I do not mind,' Mr. Creach said. 'How often does a mere solicitor get the opportunity to argue and then rest his case, like a valued barrister?'

'Since you are being so accommodating, Mr. Creach,' I said, 'was it you who ripped that photograph out in Frankham's house and attempted to destroy the frame?'

'Oh, that. No, it happened quite on the spur of the moment. You see, Mrs. Watson, the deduction you relayed to Kitty is quite right. I was in Frankham's house that night, and I did witness the argument between he and Standish. I was there to try and convince Frankham yet again to let me into the cult. When he refused, I'm afraid I lost my temper, and grabbed the picture of him in his worship garb, which he seemed so proud of, smashed the frame and tore up the photograph. Frankly, I was rather hoping that upon destroying the picture, Frankham would crumple before me and die in agonizing throes, like Dorian Gray.'

'Geoffrey, the longer we are out here, the greater the risk of discovery we are taking,' Kitty said. 'Put them in the boat.'

'Yes, it is time,' Mr. Creach said. 'Get inside the boat, Mrs. Watson.'

'And if I refuse?'

Kitty stepped forward with the pistol. 'Then we will hold your head underneath the water until you are dead and put you in the boat. Whoever finds you will not be able to tell that you were drowned before the boat went down.'

'It would, however, look a bit suspicious if Dr. Watson's wrists were still bound with rope, don't you think?' Creach said, suddenly producing a knife. He grabbed my husband and rolled him over like a sack of grain, then sawed through the ropes around his wrists. Then, rolling my moaning husband over again, he dragged John towards the edge of the water. John grunted as he was hoisted into the boat. Then Mr. Creach came back to me.

'On your feet,' he said, holding the knife threateningly.

I desperately tried to think of a way out of this, but nothing came. With overwhelming reluctance, I started to walk to the boat; and, as much as I detested profanity, I could not keep from thinking: *Damn the man!* I stepped into the craft, kneeling to cradle John's head.

'May the end come quickly for you,' Creach said, as he started to push the boat into the water.

I closed my eyes and began to pray.

And then I heard a gunshot. It had to be Kitty, since he was the one with the pistol, but at whom was he shooting? There was another shot, this one louder, and I lurched up to see what was happening. Now there were other strange noises and lights. A third gunshot caused the cab horse, which had been standing patiently throughout, to suddenly rear up and bolt, taking the hansom with it.

'Kitty, look out!' Mr. Creach shouted, and I sat up just in time to see the runaway horse collide with Kitty Cornwell and knock him down. I blanched as the hooves and wheels of the hansom passed over him.

'*No!*' Geoffrey Creach screamed, rushing towards Kitty. By that time the horse and empty cab had disappeared into the night.

I could feel the boat slowly slipping into the water, and with Creach detained, I jumped back out and pulled on the stern with all my strength, dragging it back on the bank.

Geoffrey Creach's anguished cries were now met by another voice, which said: 'What is going on here?'

Silhouetted against two bright lights, I saw the form of a man standing over the sobbing figure of Geoffrey Creach, cradling in his arms the head of Kitty Cornwell. 'Whoever you are, do not shoot!' I called. 'I am unarmed.'

'And so am I,' the standing figure called back, and immediately I recognised his voice. I then realised that the sounds I had heard, the loud explosions that had frightened the cab horse, led to Kitty Cornwell's injury, and, ultimately, saved the lives of John and myself, were not gunshots but backfires from the engine of a Vulcan Two-seater Runabout.

'Lord Beckham, it is Amelia Watson,' I cried.

'Gods, woman, you do turn up in the oddest of places!'

'As do you, thank heavens.'

'I was up in the tower with my telescope and saw a light in the woods where none should be,' he explained. 'I thought it might be that group of Cam worshippers you have been asking about, so I decided to investigate. But instead of the anticipated gathering of cultists, I find you and a bald-headed woman.'

'Please, my husband needs help!'

'We must get Kitty to a surgeon!' screamed Geoffrey Creach, cradling his lover's body.

'There is one here already, but you incapacitated him!' I screamed back.

Lord Beckham knelt down and picked up Kitty's wrist, checking it for a pulse, and then dropped it, shaking his head. 'It is too late for a surgeon.'

'Noooo!' Geoffrey Creach wailed. Then turning to his lordship cried, 'This is your fault! You had to drive up in that mechanical horror and frighten the horse! Now you will pay for Kitty's death!'

Still clutching the knife in his hand, the blade of which glinted in the light of the headlights, the solicitor charged Lord Beckham. His lordship deftly sidestepped the attack and delivered a blow to Mr. Creach's back that sent him sprawling. The knife fell from the lawyer's hand and Lord Beckham kicked it away. Then, pulling Mr. Creach up by the collar, his lordship held him face to face and said: 'I take a dim view, sir, of someone threatening me with a knife.' The solicitor began to struggle, trying to break free, but was stopped a second later by Lord Beckham's forceful upwards blow to his jaw. Mr. Creach fell limp and unconscious, and his lordship let go of him. Then, rubbing his knuckles, he turned to me and said: 'Cambridge Boxing Champion, 1871!'

'Please, you must help my husband,' I begged. 'He is drugged and lying in a boat by the river's edge.'

'I see no boat,' his lordship said.

'No … John … oh, God …'

Then I heard a faint voice calling, 'Amelia,' and saw my husband crawling up the bank!

'Oh, darling!' I said, rushing to him and practically throwing myself over him.

'Boat … started to … slide … into water … I … got out …' he moaned.

'Oh, John, thank God, thank God!'

After tying Geoffrey Creach up with the rope that had been used to fasten John's hands and feet, Lord Beckham leapt into his motorcar and headed off to summon the police. I continued to shield John until he returned, during which time Creach had awakened and was performing an annoying combination of a scream and a sob.

With the help of an officer I was able to get John into a police carriage, and return to the hotel some time after one in the morning. I pounded on the door until a nightgowned Mrs. Grimes appeared to see what the commotion was.

'Oh, I'm so sorry, dear,' she said. 'There were times when my husband, God rest his soul, used to stay out and then come back in that condition, too.'

I did not even bother to correct her as I half-dragged, half-carried John up the stairs to our room.

* * *

I awoke rather early the next morning, full of nervous energy, which I put to good use by starting to pack. It was some time after nine before John awoke with a horrendous headache.

'Great Scott,' he said, rubbing his head, 'what on earth happened to me?'

'It is quite a long story, darling,' I said. 'Do you remember anything of yesterday?'

'I remember meeting Creach at the train station and having him drag me off to a coffee shop somewhere, and then up to his office; and after that I only have strange flashes of dream memory. I can vaguely recall crawling out of a box, or maybe it was a coffin, and pulling myself along the ground. What a nightmare that must have been! And what on earth could I have been drinking to bring it on?'

'Mr. Creach slipped you some of the draught you gave to Ronnie Standish.'

'He did what? Why would he do that? Oh, Lord! I hope it hasn't affected Standish the way it has me. But really, Amelia, why would Creach do that?'

'Because he turned out to be the killer.'

'*What?*' John shouted, and then immediately regretted it. His hands over his face, he sank back onto the pillow, moaning. I took a handkerchief and rushed to the basin, wetted it, and came back to gently lay it over his brow.

'Would you like the entire story, dear?' I asked.

'Can you give me a truncated version?'

I did my best, but it still took time, chiefly because John insisted upon interrupting me every few sentences to ask questions or make a comment. By the end of the story, he had been energised enough to get out of bed and get dressed. I could see that his head was still on the tender side, but he appeared to gain functionality with each passing second. In fact, he was soon cognizant enough to notice that my bags were packed and resting by the door.

'You appear ready to check out,' he commented.

'I wish to leave Bath at once, John.'

If only it were that easy.

Reporters were waiting for us to emerge from our room, apparently having been tipped off by the police. In the front of the pack was Mr. Bryce of the *Police Gazette.* It was the better part of an hour before they left, at which time I was nearly exhausted from answering all the questions. Once the last one had been scooted out, I asked Mrs. Grimes for an uncharacteristically early glass of wine, and she was more than delighted to fetch it.

'Grand fellows, the lot of them,' she said admiringly of the press.

'I thought you did not like reporters,' I said, taking the wine glass and sipping.

'I didn't before, but once the story is out and people read how the wife of the famous Dr. Watson of London and the doctor himself solved the terrible crime, and how they did it while they were guests of the Roman, I'll be turnin' people away! 'Tis a brass plaque I'll be puttin' on the door, readin' *The Watson Room*, and 'tis extra I'll be chargin' for it, too!'

The landlady then disappeared into the back and John and I went up to get our luggage. In the room, however, I said: 'Wait, darling. Before we leave, I really should say goodbye to Bella.'

'I suppose so. I will stay here and wait for you.'

'No, John, please, I don't want to be separated from you again.'

'Very well.'

Leaving the bags in the room, we walked to Albert Street, just in time to see another locust-like swarm of reporters leaving the Standish home. PC Richter was once more outside the front to help shoo them away. We stayed hidden until they had gone and then approached him.

'How do you do, ma'am?' he said, briskly. 'I heard all about what happened last night. Dreadful. That lawyer fellow confessed to everything. Said nothing mattered now that the other bloke was dead, the one what was wearing a dress.' He shook his head. 'I'm afraid all this is beyond me.'

'Well, Mr. Creach confessed, and that is the important thing,' I said. 'I trust Bella is in?'

'Oh, yes, and the mister, too. Go right in, ma'am.'

I had no sooner opened the door than Bella practically flew into my arms. 'Oh, Amelia, I cannot thank you enough!'

Behind her was a beaming Ronnie Standish, who said, 'You have given me my life back, Mrs. Watson.'

As much as I was hoping for a hasty exit, there was no practical way to accomplish it, so we stayed and talked with the Standishes, and even ate some really dreadful sandwiches that Bella made. We would probably still be there, in fact, if not for the gunshots outside.

John and Ronnie leapt up from their chairs with alarm, while Bella crouched behind the sofa. I, meanwhile, stood up calmly and smiled, having recognised the sounds immediately. 'We are not in danger,' I said, going to the door and opening it to see Lord Beckham, resplendent in his driving coat and goggles, sitting in his rattling, smoking motorcar.

'The lady at the hotel said you'd be here,' his lordship called out.

'Thank you for coming to check on us, but we are about to leave,' I said.

'Oh, what a pity. Before you depart, though, we need to discuss the medallion.'

'The medallion? It is not mine to discuss. It belongs to the young man who lives here.'

'Where is he? I will offer any amount —'

'Great Scott!' John interrupted, as he dashed from the house and ran past me in order to view the motorcar. 'Is that the Vulcan that saved our lives last night?'

'It is indeed,' Lord Beckham replied,

'and, I daresay, that is one use the manufacturers had not envisioned.'

When Ronnie and Bella emerged from the house, his lordship leapt out of his motorcar and raised his goggles.

'You must be the young man of the medallion!' he said to Ronnie. 'How much will you take for it? Name your amount my good man.'

'It's not for sale, sir,' Ronnie replied.

'Ronnie,' Bella said, 'can't you even consider it? Think of what we could do if we had money!'

'The medallion belongs in a museum, Bella.'

'Excellent!' Lord Beckham said. 'I shall buy it and establish one. Jannah knows I already own enough relics to fill the Tower of London, but your medallion, young man, shall be the centrepiece of the collection.' He produced a calling card and handed it to Ronnie. 'We shall talk further, young man.'

'Thank you, sir,' Bella said, elbowing her husband into taking the card.

'Thank you, sir,' Ronnie repeated, dutifully.

Lord Beckham returned to his motorcar, over which John was hovering like a hawk.

'Have you ever ridden in one of these, Doctor?' his lordship asked.

'No, no, but I've wanted to.'

'Then climb in, man, climb in!'

By the time I reached the curb, both my husband and his lordship were astride the iron mule and begoggled like insects, and both waved to me as the infernal device lurched forward and spluttered down the street.

Rather than wait for them, I turned and walked back to the Roman Hotel, knowing that one way or another, the Vulcan would turn up at its door — or else the police would, informing me what part of the Avon they had plunged into. Missy had finished packing the bags and was waiting in the sitting room, along with Mrs. Grimes. Before long, the now-familiar gunshots announced the motorcar's arrival, and I shudder to relate that it was now John who was behind the wheel of the contraption!

The motorcar was all that John could talk about as we rode to the train station in a blessedly old-fashioned two-horse phaeton.

'You know, darling,' I said, hoping to change the subject, 'this really is a charming city, despite ... well, despite everything.'

A plaintive whistle sounded off in the distance, announcing the approach of the train that would take us back to smoky, cloudy, crowded, bustling London. Unfortunately, neither of us saw the suitcase directly behind me, which I tripped over, launching into a bizarre — and, alas, unsuccessful — dance to maintain my balance. I cried out as I went down hard onto the wooden platform.

'Good heavens, Amelia, are you all right?' John said, as he gently helped me up.

'Oh, John,' I moaned, 'I think I've re-sprained my ankle!'

From somewhere behind us, far off in the verdant, terraced hills, I thought I heard the sound of a god laughing.

We do hope that you have enjoyed reading this large print book.

Did you know that all of our titles are available for purchase?

We publish a wide range of high quality large print books including:

Romances, Mysteries, Classics
General Fiction
Non Fiction and Westerns

Special interest titles available in large print are:

The Little Oxford Dictionary
Music Book, Song Book
Hymn Book, Service Book

Also available from us courtesy of Oxford University Press:

Young Readers' Dictionary
(large print edition)
Young Readers' Thesaurus
(large print edition)

For further information or a free brochure, please contact us at:
Ulverscroft Large Print Books Ltd.,
The Green, Bradgate Road, Anstey,
Leicester, LE7 7FU, England.
Tel: (00 44) 0116 236 4325
Fax: (00 44) 0116 234 0205

Other titles in the
Linford Mystery Library:

DEATH WARRIORS

Denis Hughes

When geologist and big game hunter Rex Brandon sets off into the African jungle to prospect for a rare mineral, he is prepared for danger — two previous expeditions on the same mission mysteriously disappeared, never to return. But Brandon little realises what horrors his own safari will be exposed to . . . He must deal with the treachery and desertion of his own men, hunt a gorilla gone rogue, and most terrifyingly of all, face an attack by ghostly warriors in the Valley of Devils . . .

PHANTOM HOLLOW

Gerald Verner

When Tony Frost and his colleague Jack Denton arrive for a holiday at Monk's Lodge, an ancient cottage deep in the Somerset countryside, they are immediately warned off by the local villagers and a message scrawled in crimson across a windowpane: 'THERE IS DANGER. GO WHILE YOU CAN!' Tony invites his friend, the famous dramatist and criminologist Trevor Lowe, to come and help — but the investigation takes a sinister turn when the dead body of a missing estate agent is found behind a locked door in the cottage . . .

THE DEVIL IN HER

Norman Firth

The Devil In Her sees Doctor Alan Carter returning to England to stay with an old friend, Colonel Merton, after seven arduous years abroad — only to receive a terrible shock. He first encounters frightened locals who tell him tales of a ghostly woman in filmy white roaming the moors and slaughtering animals. Dismissing their warnings, he proceeds to Merton Lodge — and into a maze of mystery and death. While in *She Vamped a Strangler*, private detective Rodney Granger investigates a case of robbery and murder in the upper echelons of society.